WEDDINGS,
WEAPONS AND
a White Christmas

BY M.A. HANSEN

Cover art is designed by Mariah Sinclair, mariahsinclair.com

Prologue

"The last shipment will be next week. Make sure we have no more mistakes."

The two men stood at the edge of the parking lot, smoking cigarettes of clove and menthol. They loaded the boxes on the truck, closed the roll-down door, and padlocked it.

"If everything goes according to plan, we will have these in the hands of my comrades!"

"This is my last job. I can't be a part of this anymore. I'm done!" The young man declared.

The older man with the tattoo of the lady in red looked up from his clipboard. His eyes narrowed, and he took a puff of his cigarette. The smoke plumed off in the distance. He would not let this go!

"I pay you well! Is it more money you want?"

"No, I want to move on!"

"I see."

After the older man had considered this, he puffed on the last of his cigarettes, dropped it to the concrete, and smashed it out.

He reached into his jacket pocket and held his cold steel. He would have to cut his loose ends. He looked around the parking lot, filled with cars, for the two large events taking place: a large wedding and the Guns and Amo Convention. They were parked between many other large trucks that had products and supplies to sell or display at the convention. "Do me a solid and grab my case in the truck, will you?"

The older man asked.

The younger man walked back to the side of the truck and opened the passenger side door. Just as he bent over to grab the black case, he grunted and fell to the ground.

The older man had hit him with the end of the gun.

He cut his loose end with one shot.

Chapter 1

December 14

"Falling in love... With you..." "We should end with a drawn-out you and fade." I sang the last bar of the song, and we noted the ending. Roxi and I were rehearsing the song that I was going to sing for the happy couple for their first dance.

Diaz and Lindsey had asked me last summer if I would be willing to sing the first dance song for them.

Of course, I said yes in a heartbeat.

We began about an hour ago practicing in one of the banquet rooms at Kendle's. Roxi at the baby grand, and I sitting on a high stool I grabbed from the bar.

"All right! I think this is going to be great, now let's go eat!" Roxi said.

It was 5:30 pm, and the dinner crowd was beginning to come in.

"I could use a glass of red right now. How about you, Roxi?"

"Oh yeah!"

Roxi and I walked into the dining room by the bar to get some dinner.

"Hi, Tito, can you get two steak dinners and two glasses of Jay Lohr Cabs for us?"

"Coming right up, ladies."

Tito took our order with a smile.

"I think the wedding will be beautiful; a December wedding is so cool, I mean, it will be so Christmas-y."

"Roxi, I saw the dresses. Lindsey showed them to me last week; they are the prettiest shade of cranberry, and her gown is going to be an ivory or cream color. It looks gorgeous, plus the decor at the Huntington will be decked out for the season. I think this will be the prettiest wedding I've ever been to."

"Girl, speaking of decor, you guys did a fab job of this place."

Roxi said, looking around the restaurant this evening.

She was right, Tito, Daisy, Paul, and I put up all of the Christmas decorations and the trees on November 30 so that we were ready for December 1.

The motif this year was inspired by a White Christmas theme; I had five trees brought in. One tree in each of the banquet rooms makes three, and one tree at the entrance by the hostess's desk, and one very large one by the stage.

The color palette I decided on was a mix of white and natural wood, with touches of red. I opted for non-flocked trees and garland to look more realistic and not so kitschy!

I placed the mistletoe by the entrance to the dining room, just past the hostess desk in the lobby.

I had white lights everywhere, some twinkling and some still. The fireplace mantle had white candles in hurricane covers, with garland and white lights. I placed two tall glass jars with lids filled with pine cones and red ribbons wrapped around them.

White lighted tree branches in vases and free-standing ones as well were decorated all over the restaurant. The entrance by the hostess desk had many white and red poinsettias offering color and cheer. I had the windows here frosted around the edges to resemble a snowscape. I even came up with a cool uniform for the servers. For the men, Roxi and I came up with dark navy slacks, a white button-down dress shirt, a red Royal Stewart Tartan vest, and a dark forest green necktie.

For the gals: servers, cocktail waitresses, and hostesses, they all had a hand in this one. We decided on a retro 1950s circle skirt in red Stewart tartan, with a white petticoat underneath, a white 3/4 sleeve cotton top, and a navy blue sheer chiffon neck scarf.

Instead of high heels (I did wear them when I was a hostess at one point in my life), we all opted for a pair of navy leather Mary Janes, with a chunky short heel, and surprisingly very comfortable. Our steaks arrived, mine medium rare, and Roxi's cooked to cremation.

We toasted our Cabernets and said cheers.

"Okay, Roxi, here is to a very happy and beautiful December."

"Amen, sister!"

The baked potato was filled with all of my favorites: butter, cheese, bacon, sour cream, and chives! Oh yeah, I like it loaded!

After dinner, the band got up on stage, and we started with "Please Come Home For Christmas," followed by "Merry Christmas Darling." It's one of my favs, too!

Paul walked in and took a seat at a booth to the left of the stage. I smiled at him, and he smiled back. He came in to have a drink since he was off for the rest of the night. November had been a nice, slow month for crime, and we had some time to reconnect. Thanksgiving with his family was a new experience.

He's the youngest of five siblings, with two older sisters and two older brothers.

His two sisters, twins, are in their early 40s and married with two kids each. One of his older brothers is engaged, and the one who's just a year 1/2 older than Paul is single like he is.

It was nice meeting his parents; they were very welcoming and kind, and I got along great with them. There was no pressure, no rushing to the aisle comments. Paul introduced me as his friend, and that was it; no boundaries were crossed, and no questions were asked.

They were all wonderful. A house full of football fans who love to eat. I fit in like a glove. Paul's parents moved to Lake Havasu in Arizona, but his siblings are still here in California. We spent Thanksgiving weekend on a pontoon boat around the lake, took in some nice warm temps, and sat beneath the many stars above.

We finished our show for the evening, and so I had a drink waiting for me at the bar afterward.

"Hi, did you have a nice day, honey?" He asked me, a sweet grin on his face.

I sat down next to him and smiled,

"The best." I took a drink of my Cherry Coke over crushed ice with a maraschino cherry on top.

My cell phone chimed a tune of "Rock n' Around the Christmas Tree" by Brenda Lee.

I know it's old school to have ringtones, but what can I say, I'm a musician, I love music.

"Hello, Lindsey."

"Nikki! I'm sorry to call you so late, but my cousin just called me. She is in the Navy, and she has orders to fly out tonight with her team for a special mission. That's all I know. It's classified, but she was going to be a bridesmaid at the wedding, and now we are down one person! I hate to ask, but could you possibly fill in for her? Oh, please!"

"Of course, I will! Don't worry, ok."

"Oh, I'm so relieved! Thank you! I know you will fit in the dress, you and my cousin are the same size. An eight, right?"

"Yes, that's my size."

"Perfect, we have a rehearsal the day before at the church at 4:30 pm, can you make it?"

"No problem, I'll be there Friday night."

"Thank you, Nikki, you don't know how much this means to me."

"I'm glad I was able to help Lindsey."

"Ok, I'll see you Friday, and I will bring the dress too. Thank you again, bye."

"Bye, Lindsey."

I hung up my phone and slipped it into my back pocket.

"Guess what, Paul? I'm in the wedding."

"You'll be a beautiful bridesmaid."

"Thank you."

We finished our drinks and left Kendle's. Paul drove me home. I had walked over earlier today, and the bug was parked at my place. Paul came in for some tea and dessert. Earlier this evening, he went to the annual *City Employee Holiday Bash*. The city has this every year for city workers, law enforcement, and first responders. The band played a few times over the years, but tonight, they hired a DJ because we have been so busy at Kendle's. Two of the girls caught the flu, and I just didn't have the availability.

"I saw Matt at the city party tonight."

"Yeah, he asked me to go with him," I said, putting the kettle on the stove.

Paul looked at me; his expression was unsettled.

"Are you serious?"

"Yes, I know we haven't had a chance to talk about this, but how about now?"

He sat on the couch, and I walked around the room but got right to it.

"Matt told me he wants to get back together. Last month, he told me he would wait until I was ready for a serious commitment."

"He does know that we are dating and that we are in a relationship?"

I could see Paul getting upset now.

"Yes! I did explain to him that I am dating you and only you at this time."

"I wish you had told me sooner; I would've had a man-to-man conversation with him."

Oh boy, now I did it, here comes the testosterone!

"Maybe I should have had a conversation with Stacie when she planted that kiss on you."

My hands on my hips now.

He settled down now and regrouped.

"I see your point. I won't have any *discussions* with him."

He reassured me.

I eased up and sat next to him on the sofa.

"Part of this is my fault; when we started dating, we had both agreed we were not ready for a committed relationship. I broke up with Matt because we were moving too fast, and that freaked me out. Then, when I met you and we started dating, it was fun and exciting, and you weren't pulling me down the aisle of marriage.

I felt at ease with you, calm. Now, at this point, I guess I'm wondering where we stand. Are we now committed to each other, or do we still have no strings attached?"

"I guess this part is my fault. When we went to see my family for Thanksgiving, I introduced you as my *friend*, but I see our relationship is progressing to another level, and you're right: when we first started dating, I *did* say I didn't want a commitment! I had too many women I dated pushing me down the aisle, too! My job is very demanding, and I'm not always there, it led to a lot of breakups and cheating girlfriends for me. I guess what I'm saying is that with you, it's different; we both want to take it slow and not rush into anything."

He stood up right in front of me. Looking deep into my eyes.

"So I'm asking you, are you ready for the next step?"

But before I could answer, he said,

"Because I am." He looked confident and pleased with his choice, a metamorphosis of his relationship with me.

I went silent!

Chapter 2

December 18

The Wedding

The day was sunny with a rift of cool air; the weather was predicted to be a comfortable 72 degrees. The church was packed with guests; the string quartet was playing Pachelbel, Canon in D major. Sunlight streamed in through the beautiful vintage stained glass windows. The four of us ladies were walking down the aisle with our groomsmen in our cranberry red, off-the-shoulder gowns, pearl earrings, and matching necklaces, a gift from the bride. Our strides were slow to keep step with the music until we reached the front of the church, where we paired off to the left, and the groomsmen went right. Jason (Jay to his friends) Diaz stood proud; his black tuxedo and fabulous smile looked like a million bucks. His best man was right by his side, another brother from the blue. Paul smiled at me from his seat five rows back; he looked incredibly handsome in his navy blue suit.

The music ended, and the quartet began with the song

"A Thousand Years" by Christina Perri.

Lindsey stood at the church doors with her father. She wore a long ivory ball gown in satin, off-the-shoulder long lace sleeves, and a bodice with a sweetheart neckline. The satin sash at the waistline had pearls and sparkling mock diamonds.

A beautiful lace veil cascaded down from her dark hair, lavish with large curls, and it was put up in a low bun at the nape of the neck, dotted with pearls. Inspired by Grace Kelley and Kate Middleton's gowns, she looked amazing!

The guests stood for the bride's entrance, and many women began to cry and dabbed at their eyes.

By the time Lindsey reached Jay, his eyes were watery with love. The two joined hands and said their vows, exchanged rings, and bound together with the lasso. (A tradition in Mexican Catholic wedding ceremonies, the wedding lasso is a large rosary, placed around the couple as a symbol of unity.)

The priest, Father Riley, now said: "I pronounce you Mr. and Mrs. Jason Diaz. You may kiss the bride."

Everyone clapped for them, the violinist began to play Pachelbel once again, and Jay and Lindsey led the way out of the church, with the bridesmaids and groomsmen following them.

It was a short drive to the reception at the Huntington Hotel in Rancho Niguel. The wedding party climbed into the waiting white Cadillac SUVs that were decorated with cranberry-colored paper flowers. Also, an ode to Mexican wedding traditions that Jay and Lindsey wanted to have.

The bride and groom left ahead of us in a white Rolls-Royce. We were all to meet up at the hotel gardens for photos. The gardens at the Huntington were bordering on paradise. I don't know who designed it, but man, I hope heaven is this beautiful. Two large Lilly ponds with blooming flowers and bright green Lilly pads set the scene. Swans gliding about the pond, delicate with grand poise. A large rose garden with a tall marble gazebo with an iron dome of swirls and hearts. A large green lawn with small marble benches here and there. We took photos all around the grounds; we took some next to a man-made waterfall that rushed over granite rock and simmered down into a pool on the south lawn of the property. Streams with lovely little bridges and eucalyptus trees all around. Trellises open to more paths of cobblestone bordered with wildflowers. A grand estate, it was much like an East Coast old money mansion, built by some conglomerate, the Rockefellers, or the Vanderbilts, pretty much any wealthy man who was on the Titanic kind of estate. It was fancy!

After many fun photos, we walked up to the hotel and headed to the banquet room. Before entering, we lined up in the outer hall, waiting to be announced by the DJ upon our entrance.

Jay and Lindsey were at the back of the line; they were happy and very overjoyed. The day had been a very nice one, clear and blue skies, the high reaching up to 74 degrees. You hardly realized it was December, but that's SoCal. The hotel was decorated with green garland that held gold bulb ornaments and white ribbons. The lobby held a very tall Christmas tree with white lights and glittery ornaments, and bulbs in gold. In the ballroom, next door, down the hall on the west side of the building, was a convention of Guns and Ammo. Many individuals had jackets with the names of company sponsors, gun companies, hunting clothing companies, and different companies that make supplies for avid game and arms enthusiasts.

The ballroom doors opened, and the DJ announced the first two couples, and they walked inside the room. I was next with Jay's cousin as my partner. We walked in with smiles from ear to ear and danced to the song "Let's Get it Started" From The Black Eyed Peas.

The room was spectacular, with crystal chandeliers and tall floor-to-ceiling windows. White tablecloths, white napkins, and gold and white plates. Wine glasses and water goblets with gold-lined rims, florals of cranberry red roses and white peonies, with green ivy altogether in a round short vase. Small gold picture frames carried the number of the table. White votive candles burning bright in crystal glasses. White twinkle lights surrounded the many white trees in the room to give the look of a snow-filled forest. I took my seat at the reserved table with the rest of the wedding party.

I spotted Paul sitting with Detective Sonya Smith and her daughter, Anita. To his right, Craig and Kiana sat clapping along with the music. Roxi and her date were the last two seated with Paul. All the guests were smiling and cheering. It was now time to introduce the happy newlyweds.

"Ladies and gentlemen, if I can get everyone to stand up, it's time to introduce the happy couple. Mr. & Mrs. Jason Diaz!"

Lindsey and Jay entered the room hand in hand, with a few kisses in there. The song "Walking on Sunshine" by Katrina and the Waves played.

Everyone cheered, a few whistles were heard throughout the room, and the couple took their seats at the head of the long table the bridal party sat. The servers came right out and began at our table. Lindsey and Jay were the first served.

Caesar salad, prime rib with fresh sautéed veggies, whipped mashed potatoes, and rolls and butter. Our table had two vegetarian dishes of eggplant parmesan and one fish meal.

I, of course, the carnivore that I am, had the prime rib.

The food was fantastic! Oh my, I put a little horseradish on my meat and indulged.

As soon as the rest of the room was served, the toasts began. Lindsey's parents had a sweet speech with tears, and Jay's parents followed with the same. The Best man and the Maid of honor made their speeches, sharing some cute memories of the couple as well.

After dinner, I headed to the ladies' room to freshen up. On my way through the hall to the restrooms, I saw two men discussing something that made one of them, the one with a black ball cap with the words Rancho Raiders, turn away from me when I passed by. Hmmm, that was strange, I thought to myself.

The ladies' room was, oh my gosh, stunning!

A nice powder room area complete with a vanity table, tissues, perfumes, and complementary makeup removers in glass jars.

I had my small dental kit with a travel toothbrush, paste, and floss. I didn't want to end up with prime rib in my teeth.

After I brushed and flossed, reapplied my lipstick, and checked my appearance in the gold 8-foot full-length mirror.

I walked back out to the hall; Paul was waiting for me.

"You look amazing in that dress, Nikki."

"Thank you. You look pretty darn good, too!"

He went in for a kiss, but I had to stop him this time.

"I have to go on stage right now, I can't smudge my lipstick."

"Ok, but later, though, when the dancing starts."

He smiled with those shining green eyes.

We walked back to the banquet room, I took my seat, and Paul went back to his table.

"Now, let's have the bride and groom up here for their first dance." The DJ announced.

Roxi and I made our way to the side of the dance floor by the bar where the white baby grand piano stood.

She sat down to play, and I took the mic. Jay and Lindsey were on the dance floor now.

Roxi played the intro, and I sang, "I can't help falling in love with you." By the late great king of rock n' roll and one of my personal favorites, Elvis Presley.

The tears were rolling down Lindsey's face, and Jay kissed them away. Next, a round of applause came from their friends and family.

The DJ clapped and remarked, "That was just beautiful. Let's give a round of applause for Nikki Rodriguez and Roxi Carmichael!"

The room erupted in applause, Jay and Lindsey applauded too, and mouthed thank yous.

"It's time to get the party started!" The DJ shouted and played "DJ's Got Us Falling In Love Again" mixed with "Give Me Everything Tonight" by Pitbull, dancing music.

Paul and I started to cut a rug, the dance floor now full with everyone celebrating and letting loose. Roxi and her beau danced like pros. The next song, a throwback to the 70s-80s, "September" by Earth, Wind, and Fire.

After the song, the cake cutting commenced; no super messes here, Jay and Lindsey were nice to one another, but Lindsey did get frosting on Jay's nose, then she kissed him. The guests were having a blast, and after some chocolate and raspberry-filled cake, the dance floor wasn't empty.

Paul and I stole away through a patio door that led out to a terrace. "Finally, we're alone."

Paul pulled me into an embrace. We kissed, and he held me close. I could hear "Oh My God" by Usher playing and the guests cheering, "oh oh oh oh oh my God..." The guests were shouting!

"Sounds like they're getting crazy in there!" Paul remarked.

"Let's go back in!" I smiled.

We walked back into the banquet room and joined the party...

After dancing a few fast dances, the DJ slowed it down!

"Grab your sweetheart and settle in for a nice slow dance." The DJ announced.

He played the song "Remember When" By Alan Jackson. I rested my head on Paul's shoulder, his heart beating fast from dancing, now slowing down as we swayed in each other's arms.

"I don't want this night to end."

He whispered.

I couldn't have said it better. Paul and I made a nice couple, and my feelings for him were becoming deeper.

"It is pretty great!" I responded.

The song soon ended, and the light brightened.

"All right, ladies and gentlemen, it's time for the bouquet and garter toss! All of you single gals and single guys, get on up here!" The DJ, with his loud and fun voice, shouted.

"Are you going out there?" Paul asked.

"No way!" I laughed.

"I'm not going up there," Paul remarked.

We went to the corner of the room and sort of hid from the many ladies rushing onto the dance floor to go and catch Lindsey's bouquet.

"I think we will be safe here." I laughed as we hid out.

The DJ came back on the mic.

"Can we have Nikki Rodriguez up here? Nikki, where are you?"

I had a look of shock on my face.

"No way!"

Paul laughed, "I guess you're wanted up there!"

The DJ then said.

"Can we also get Paul Anderson up here for the garter toss, too!"

I laughed as I saw Paul's face turn green.

"Oh no, not me too!"

We laughed with each other, and then the spotlight found us, and so did the DJ.

"Come on, you two, we are waiting."

We walked up towards the dance floor; Paul stood back as I walked on the dance floor with many other ladies, eager to catch the bouquet.

They were cracking their knuckles and stretching their arms, poising themselves with a stable stance, and they were like a bunch of thoroughbreds at the starting gate, ready to be released.

Lindsey was standing a few feet in front of us.

She smiled at me, and I took my place behind the front line of gals.

Roxi stood out front with the others, ready to go.

In one, two, and three, Lindsey threw the bouquet; it shot back, it was headed right for me, I was a deer in headlights; my brow was sweating, and my arms reluctantly trying to raise above my head to catch it.

Then, all of a sudden, two arms shot in front of me, and a tall blond grabbed the bouquet and hugged it close to her chest. Whew! Thank God, I did a little happy dance and smiled, and clapped for her.

She was so excited that she ran to Lindsey and hugged her.

I dodged that bullet.

Next was the garter toss. Jay stood out front with about 20 unwilling guys behind him, Paul's face a look of fear! Jay shot the baby blue garter in the air; it went over Paul and landed on a cute Latino dude, Jay's cousin, I believe.

He was a good sport; he held it up in the air and did a fist bump with Jason. Paul looked relieved.

"I guess it's a good thing neither one of us wants to marry the other." I winked at him.

"Well, maybe someday."

He smiled and pulled me in for a kiss.

The music started again, and the guests filled the dance floor with another great dance hit, "Don't Stop Until You Get Enough," by another one of my favs, the late great king of pop, Michael Jackson.

Paul and I headed outside for some fresh air.

It was a little warm, and the cool air felt great. We took a walk along the cobblestone path and found our way to the pond; we lingered there for a while. It wasn't that late, only 6:45 pm, and we could hear the music going in the distance. We kissed again and made some small talk and kissed, and then we heard it!

A scream in the distance broke our embrace, and now we ran to the excitement. We were not too far from the parking lot; I saw a woman standing by a body on the floor by a white moving truck. Paul flashed his badge, and I took the distraught woman away from the scene. He dialed 911, and we could hear the sirens coming a few minutes later.

"The Party is over,"

Paul said.

Chapter 3

Later that same night

The victim was male, in his late 30s, and an employee of Rancho Arms and Tactical. A small gun store a few miles from the hotel, out on Route 66.

"Right now, it's preliminary, but it looks like a gunshot is what killed him. I have to wait for the coroner's call on this, but it's a homicide!"

The wedding was over, and it was a good thing that Jay and Lindsey had no idea what was going on. They were leaving the hotel on the opposite side of the back entrance. They were given an awesome send-off; they climbed into the Rolls and drove away with fireworks going off up above. They had an early flight at 5:45 am to Hawaii, first class, a gift from all of the 87 officers at the police department. Bon Voyage Travel Agency gave the officers a good deal: a 5-day stay at the Grand Wailea Hotel, car rental, and airfare.

All of the guests cheered them on as they drove off. Many of the guests went home, and some out-of-town ones went back to the hotel, where they had a room for the evening.

A few of the officers, Craig, Sonya, and two others, went to assist Paul with the crime scene.

The Guns and Ammo Convention was over, and now many people were leaving the parking lot. The police corded off a circumference around the crime scene, a few cars were parked in that circumference, and guests and vendors of the show were interviewed by the police.

One vendor had a cart full of his supplies; he stopped by the crime scene trying to get to his grey Dodge Ram Truck.

"What happened?"

He asked one of the cops; Paul came over to him.

"I'm Detective Anderson. Is this your vehicle?"

Paul pointed to the Truck, "Yes, I'm a vendor at the convention. I own Rancho Arms and Tactical."

"Follow me," Paul told the man.

They went to the back of the coroner's van.

"Do you know this man?"

The man looked at the victim in the body bag that had been unzipped to show the victim's face.

"Oh my God, that's Ivan Smirnov, he works for me. He was running the store today; we closed at 3 pm, and he was supposed to come back here and relieve me for the rest of the convention this evening."

The store owner was distraught, and now he sat down on the sidewalk to collect himself.

Paul walked over to Craig and whispered something to him. They both nodded, and then Paul walked over to Sonya. He conversed with her, and they nodded again. Confirming something that only they knew.

The body was taken away by the coroner, and now the crime scene forensic team was doing their job.

The owner of the store collected himself, and Paul was taking down his information. He began to interview him by asking questions about the employee.

How long has he worked for him? How long did he know him? Did he have any family? Does he have any enemies?

These are the usual questions a detective asks while investigating a murder.

I found Roxi and her date, and I asked for a ride home with them. I had originally arrived with Paul earlier in the day, so he was my transportation, but he was going to be a while.

On the way home, Roxi asked me what happened.

"Paul and I were outside getting some fresh air when all of a sudden we heard a woman scream, and so we went to the scream and then found a body."

"Just when I thought the holidays were off to a good start, then this," Roxi said.

" Now that Paul is on this case, he will be pretty busy again; I was hoping this month would be an easy one. Especially with Christmas almost here."

Roxi and her date walked me to my door, "Thanks for the ride, guys." I hugged Roxi, and I let myself in.

Chapter 4

Say it Ain't Santa

I woke up early the next morning. It was 6 am, and I took a swim in the pool at my complex, a few laps, some butterflies, and a lap of backstroke. The pool is heated during the cold months, but this morning, it was 72 degrees; no doubt we were having warm weather. I love an outdoor pool, the fresh air, the blue sky, and the sun rising above. I think this is the best time for a swim.

After an hour, I was ready to go back to my place. I got out and dried off. I spotted Craig coming in the gate to the pool.

"Hi Craig, I'm surprised you're up this early, considering how long the investigation lasted last night."

"Hi, Nikki! Oh yeah, we didn't get out of there until about 10:30 pm, and then we went to the victims' place to search for clues. I guess I went to bed at about 12:45 or so, but that's ok, I'm always up at this hour. Anderson and I have been partnered up on the case."

He casually stated, setting his towel down on a patio chair.

"So, do you guys have any new information about the murder?"

I asked.

"Not much yet!"

Craig removed his Ray-Ban sunglasses and set them down next to the towel.

"Did it have anything to do with the Guns and Ammunition convention?"

I asked, fishing for details.

"Not really, he was an employee of the gun shop, you knew that already, but all we know about him is where he worked and lived, and that he recently came into a lot of dough!"

He removed his shirt, placed it on the towel, and slipped off his black Nike flip-flops. He stood tall and flexed his biceps, his pecks, and his forearms. Clearly, Craig is still in love with himself!

"Really, how much money?"

"20k, give or take a few hundred; it was stashed in his mattress."

I whistled a long whirrrrr sound.

Shocked at the amount of money they found.

"Yup, and if that wasn't enough, we also found a stash of guns at his place. It's looking like he was into some shady stuff."

"So, most likely, that's what got him killed!"

"Meh, probably."

Craig was ready to dive into the pool, but then stopped. He turned to me and asked.

"Hey, Nikki! Are you a Christmas Angel yet?"

"What's that?" I asked, feeling clueless.

Craig smiled.

"The department is giving a group home of kids some gifts and clothing, and each officer is looking for sponsors to pay for the donations, a Christmas Angel.

How about you be my sponsor? I figure you're good for a couple of grand! The top officer's donation gets two more weeks of vacation time. So what do you say?"

I thought fast; here he was again, trying to get me to buy something, although it was a good cause, and I would like to be a Christmas Angel, but for Paul, not Craig.

"I'm going to be Paul's Christmas Angel."

"He already has a Christmas Angel, he told me last night."

Craig said, smiling now.

"So you're stuck with old Craig! It is a good cause, and you wouldn't want your community to think you aren't charitable, right, Nikki? You have a reputation to uphold!"

He chastised me, pointing a finger toward me.

What! Ack, now he's trying to guilt me, uhh, the man has no boundaries.

I thought this through: if Paul already had a Christmas Angel, then I guess I had no other option, I did want to give to this charity, anything for kids.

"Sure, Craig, I'll be your Christmas Angel, how about $2500.00?"

"Perfect, Nikki, I knew you were good for it."

He did a little happy dance and snapped his fingers to a beat only he heard.

"I'm in first place; everyone else's bid hasn't gone past $500.00. Thanks, Nikki!"

He dived into the pool with gusto.

My mouth hung open, and my anger was escalating.

He did it again...

I threw his T-shirt in the pool. I considered the sunglasses as well, but I knew they were a gift from Kiana, and it wasn't her fault her guy was a low-down sneak.

I tied my white sarong around my waist over my white bikini bottom, put on my Gucci sunglasses and my white flip-flops, and walked off with my towel under my arm.

I left the pool area, my wet hair dripping small drops down my back. I unraveled my towel and dried my back and the bottom of my hair. My mind was racing; I had some new evidence on the murder, and the victim had a stash of money. Was this what got him killed?

I was deep in thought and halfway to my unit when I heard my name being called.

"Nikki!"

I turned around to see Matt rolling up in his red Ford F250 truck.

"Hi,"

"Get in; I'll take you back to your place."

I hopped in the passenger seat.

"So what are you doing here?"

" I was going to come by and take you to breakfast."

"Aw, that's so nice of you." I smiled.

He parked in a visitor's spot, and we went to my place.

"So, have you heard about the murder at the Huntington last night?"

"I was there! Jason and Lindsey got married yesterday; I was the second person on the scene. I consoled the woman who found him." I told Matt.

"Wow! Oh, that's right, I almost forgot, the wedding, I bet your song was fantastic."

"I did all right." I modestly admitted.

"I'm sure you were better than all right." He said, taking a seat on the sofa. I smiled and said Thank you.

"Let me just shower, and then we can go."

"You can go in your white bikini, no complaints from me."
He joked.

"Ha ha, that's cute, I'll be right back,"
I commented, heading for my room.

I showered, dried my hair quickly, and put on a pair of jeans, a halter top in dark green, and my jean jacket. I slipped on my tan sandals with a chunky heel and my tan purse.

"I'm ready."
I locked up, and we were off.

We took Matt's truck and drove to Pastries of Paris in the mall, the best French toast I've ever had. We parked on the street a few stores down and walked to the patio of the restaurant.

Once we were seated, we started with a cup of French-pressed coffee. The waitress in her black beret and black and white striped shirt took my order of French Toast Supreme with a side of bacon, and Matt ordered the big Parisian breakfast, three scrambled eggs, four sausage links, country breakfast potatoes, and a side of pancakes.

"So, tell me, what were you so upset about this morning?"

Matt asked me.

I took a sip of my coffee and then told him about my conversation with Craig, only the Christmas angel part, not the investigation part.

"So he conned me again, but it is for a good cause,"

I stated, feeling good, at least about the donation part.

We sat facing Main Street by the Pottery Barn, Coco Jo's, and many other stores down the street.

I heard a few people yell,

"Oh my gosh!"

Matt and I suddenly noticed what all of the commotion was about: a guy in a Santa hat and black hiking boots, and only those two items of clothing! He ran right in front of all of the diners on the patio and the shoppers on the sidewalk, and he ran down the street yelling **MERRY CHRISTMAS**!

Matt and I were shocked, but then we started laughing like everyone else.

The waitress set down our plates. She shook her head and said, "He's at it again, that guy has been up and down the street since yesterday!"

"What! No way!" I said.

"Oh yes!"

She replied, shaking her head in disappointment.

"I'd better call the authorities!"

She walked away, saying!

We went back to our breakfast, I took a big bite of perfectly golden French toast with powdered sugar lightly dusted and real maple syrup drizzled over it, a dollop of fresh whipped cream, and oh boy, was I in breakfast heaven.

Matt had a few big bites and complimented how wonderful his breakfast tasted. He finished what was in his mouth and reached into his back pocket.

"Nikki, I was wondering if you could keep this key for me?"

Matt asked as he handed me a gold key.

"What is this for?"

"It's a key to my house; I wanted to give it to someone I can trust in case I have an emergency or something."

"Thank you, Matt, I promise not to go through your underwear drawer." I joked.

"Ha, ha! No!" He joked, but then became serious.

"It's in case anything happens to me or if I'm out of town, and I need you to check on the place for me. I still have your key, only if you want me to."

"Of course, Matt, we both trust each other, and we are very good friends. It's a good idea, for emergency purposes or to check on each other, please hold onto my key too."

"Thank you."

He responded,

"Nikki, if you ever want to use my pool to avoid Craig, by all means, go right ahead; it's no problem."

"Thanks, I might just do that." I winked at him.

The streaker rounded the corner and came by again, but just as he passed us, a black Dodge Charger stopped in front of our patio. Paul came out of the car with sunglasses on, dark jeans, and a black polo shirt.

He radioed a unit that was up the street, and two uniformed officers took off on foot to chase the Santa streaker.

Paul saw me instantly and walked up to our table.

"Good morning, Nikki!"

"Good morning, Paul. The day is already off to a good start, huh?"

"Yeah, this is the fifth call we received about Santa. Matt, how's it going?"

"Couldn't be better, Detective Anderson."

He said, smiling from ear to ear.

"That's a pretty big breakfast you've got there, are you carb-overloading?"

"I work out, so I can afford to eat like this, but I guess some people can't." Matt looked at Paul as he replied.

"Some people don't want all of the cholesterol that comes with food like that." Paul chimed back.

That was a snide comment from Matt, considering Paul was in fantastic shape. Softballs for biceps, strong forearms, a stomach wall, toned legs, and muscled thighs. Paul was a role model for Men's Health magazine for sure.

Paul gave me a strange look; I wasn't sure if he was upset or just irritated by Matt's presence. I didn't even realize that I still had Matt's key in my hand. I put it in my purse right away.

"Paul, what's new with the case?"

"I'm still investigating."

That was all he said; he seemed very short with his answers with me now.

"I hope you find the killer soon, Craig said, you also found a lot of money, too!"

"Craig should keep his mouth shut!"

Matt looked surprised by Paul's tone, stopped eating his breakfast, and turned to Paul.

"Maybe you need some carbs; it might help your personality."

Matt shot back.

Paul returned with a comment.

"Maybe all of that sugar has gone to your head, and it's affecting your judgment!"

"Maybe your lack of sugar is affecting your manners!"

Matt returned.

The two of them were already spitting cotton at each other; the apes were pounding their chest again, and I had to stop these two fast. Neither one heard me when I said,

 "Ok, let's settle down."

I was completely ignored! A few diners on the patio were watching and enjoying this male spectacle that was playing out before them. I was just about finished with my breakfast, and I realized I needed to get away from these two. Before Matt or Paul could say anything again, I got up out of my seat.

"Matt, I'm sorry to eat and run, but I need to get going. I'm late meeting Oliver and Martin, thank you for breakfast."

I didn't give him time to object.

I picked up my purse and left.

The two of them said something to one another, but I couldn't hear what it was!

I was angry at both of them now, such men, ugg!!

I walked down Main Street and headed to the art gallery. Martin and Oliver would be an excellent ear to lend me, and they would most likely have the best advice.

I walk fast when I am angry, so

I was one door down from their entrance when I heard a car stop with a screech, and Paul stopped me.

"Nikki, please, can we talk?" He stood in front of me,

I sighed and agreed.

"Fine."

"I'm sorry, I know I came off like a jerk."

Those green eyes pleading for forgiveness.

"I saw Matt with you, and I didn't like it." He admitted.

"We were just having breakfast; it wasn't a date."

"Can we start the day over?" He asked.

I sighed.

42

"Ok, you're forgiven," I responded.

We walked into Dunner Art Gallery, and Lindo, the part-time employee, was at the front desk on the phone. He signaled to us to wait just a moment.

"Oliver, I can't find that receipt!"

I heard Martin saying.

Lindo got off the phone and said, "Zer in ze basement!"

Paul and I walked past the break room and into the back room. To the right was a staircase to the basement.

Martin was on the top step, holding a box and telling Oliver he had found it.

"Oh, Hi guys, I didn't hear you come back."

"I just came for a quick visit, Martin," I told him

"I'm here officially, Martin," Paul added, not looking forward to his visit.

"What?" I asked Paul.

Oliver came running up the stairs from the basement. He heard what Paul said, and he frowned.

"What's going on, Paul?"

"Can we go somewhere private to talk?"

"Let's go to the office." Martin led the way.

"Nikki, you should wait outside the office," Paul asked, turning to me.

"It's ok, Paul, Nikki can stay," Martin replied.

Oliver and Martin sat at their desks, and Paul and I took a seat in the visitors' chairs.

"So what is this about?"

Martin asked.

"I'm sure you heard about the murder of Ivan Smirnov, the man who was killed in the parking lot of the Huntington Hotel last night."

"Yes, Martin and I read about it this morning in the paper. What does it have to do with us?"

Oliver wanted to know.

Paul looked disappointed that he was even here discussing this, but he went on.

"The victim had a business card from your gallery and circled your address on the front of the card. He also scribbled a date and time on it.

When I was at his home, we had a team of officers searching, and they found an empty box with your address on it and some art sculptures. I was wondering if he had recently purchased anything here?"

Martin and Oliver exchanged glances and shook their heads.

"We are very close with our customers; nothing goes on that we don't know about in the store.

I can't recall anyone with that name purchasing anything here."

Oliver told Paul.

"Ok, how about anyone trying to sell you some art?"

Paul asked.

"No, we haven't had anyone new, just our regular artist.

Paul, you mentioned some sculptures, what kind of sculptures?"

Martin asked.

Looking back over his notes, Paul read.

"We found four Azteca vases, three Montezuma masks, and three mini sculptures of Aztec pyramids."

Martin and Oliver looked shocked.

"Those are due to arrive next week. What was he doing with our shipment?"

They both had concerned looks on their tanned faces.

Paul closed his black notebook, stood up, and checked his phone, which vibrated. He made a face that told me he was surprised to see this text message someone had sent him.

"Martin, that's what I'm trying to find out. If your shipment is now considered stolen, we should make sure we have a full report on it, and for your insurance as well."

Paul told them.

"I'll call our insurance company, Martin."

Oliver picked up the desk phone and began to dial.

Paul put his phone in his back pocket,

"That's all for right now, guys, but I will most likely have more questions for you later. I'll call you when I do."

I got up, too, and followed Paul out of the office.

"Is someone trying to hurt my friends?"

We were in the hallway now, just the two of us.

"Nikki, I think the art gallery is accidentally mixed up in this for some strange reason. I have a few more things to follow up on, but for right now, it looks like Ivan probably stole these shipments from the gallery."

"Matin and Oliver are completely innocent; they had nothing to do with this!"

"I know, Nikki. I don't think Martin and Oliver had anything to do with this individual either, but I have to follow the evidence."

He was very matter-of-fact.

"Is there anything I can do to help?"

I pleaded.

"I need you to let me be the detective?"

"Ok, I'm sorry, I'm just a little upset by all of this."

He rubbed my arm.

"Don't worry, it will be ok."

We walked out of the gallery.

"I'm going to get to the bottom of this. I don't want you to worry about it!"

He pulled me close, and we went in for a kiss, but we were interrupted by another "**MERRY CHRISTMAS**!"

The streaker ran right past us, across the street! Some teens were filming him on their phones, and store owners and customers came running out of the stores to catch a glimpse of the Santa Streaker!

I have to say he was pretty fast.

Paul rolled his eyes, sighed, and said, "Not today!"

He waved bye to me, got in his black police cruiser, and drove off.

Chapter 5

Girls Night Out

After leaving Martin and Oliver's gallery, I ran over to do some Christmas shopping. My mind was also on the Annual Kendle's Christmas Ball next week.

I had asked Paul to be my date for that evening, and he said yes.

We were connecting now, and I guess, looking at the situation from his point of view, my breakfast with Matt wasn't such a good idea.

I would have to put more distance between Matt and me.

We had been friends for so long that I guess I didn't think there was anything wrong with it. My relationship with Paul was going great, and I didn't want to mess it up!

As for the Christmas Ball, usually, it's a ticketed event with dinner and dancing open to the community.

We have a Santa that collects gifts for kids; we have a raffle to win a large prize, and a dance contest.

This year, I wanted to jazz it up a bit. I thought of adding some performers and a few dancers, just like in the movie "White Christmas," where they sing and dance to Christmas songs.

I also thought of having a silent auction for charity; those usually bring in a lot of money. My passion for classic movies was my motivation for these ideas. So last month, I put everything into motion, and our ticket sales are almost sold out.

The banquet room at Kendle's, the largest one, will hold 230 guests with the patio terrace included. I decided to tent the terrace in case the weather is too cold, and we have heaters that will be set up as well.

I think it's going to be the best event Kendle's ever had.

I stopped in to check out the Christmas bakeware at Coco Jo's Kitchen and Gift Shop. She's been open for a few months now after William Sonoma closed this location and went to Palm Springs.

I was so happy to know another kitchen store was still in this mall; it is my favorite so far! They have cooking tools, pots, pans, gadgets, very cute kitchen towels, aprons, cutlery, beautiful platters, bowls, mixers, gourmet food, and much more.

The place resembles a quaint shop from an age long ago, the mid-century era, if I'm guessing correctly. Hardwood floors, a brick wall, an old-fashioned cash register(only for display), a wood counter, and white shelves on the walls.

Large baskets with kitchen linens, large glass jars filled with candy sold by the 1/2 pound, on an antique buffet hutch. A front window display with a table filled with Santa and reindeer place settings and glasses. It's adorable!

I walked in to see that they were sampling peppermint bark candy on a table by the entrance, oh my! It was divine!

The store's owner, Joanne, was standing behind the register, folding aprons with snowmen and pine trees on them.

"Hi Joanne, how are you today?"

"Oh, hi Nikki, I was just thinking about you five minutes ago, it was about the Christmas Ball at Kendle's. I finally bought my tickets this morning, and my husband and I can't wait to go."

"That's wonderful to hear. You and your husband will have a blast, I promise."

"I'm sure we will, now, what can I help you with today?"

"Oh, you know, just getting my last-minute Christmas gifts and trying to steer clear of the Santa Streaker!"

She chuckled a bit, stopped her folding, and came out from behind the counter.

"Word has it that the cops haven't caught him yet. What a hoot, can you believe that guy? I mean, what is his motivation? Hey, everyone, look at what a total idiot I am."

She tossed her hand as if she was not buying it, she put her hands on her hips, and continued her comment.

"I think the guy is scaring all of the kids, I mean, seriously, can you imagine what parents are having to tell their children seeing a guy with no clothes on running through the mall, despicable, it just ain't fittin', I say!"

"You're right, I do feel bad for the kids, they will be scared looking at that guy, but here's the weird thing: you can't see anything from the waist down, it's almost as if he's wearing flesh-colored underwear!" I stated.

Joanne laughed and replied, "Yeah, you know something, you're right!" She thought for a moment but then said:

"But he's not doing anyone any favors by being naked and running around!"

She added to her comment.

I agreed!

The bell above the door chimed, and two customers walked in, a young couple in their teens.

"Well, Nikki, I'd better get back to work. Let me know if you need any help with anything here. We have 40% off on our linens today. I know how much you love our kitchen towels."

She smiled.

"Thank you. I'm going to check them out."

I walked towards the racks with the kitchen towels.

I noticed the couple walking around; they seemed off.

Joanne greeted them, "Hey, ya'll, how are you two today? Is there anything I can help you with?" Joanne was originally from South Carolina and still had her southern accent. I thought it sounded cool. I love how she says ya'll and draws it out. So cool!

The couple shook their heads,

"No, ma'am, we are just looking, thank you."

Joanne went back to her aprons, and I studied the couple from behind the rack of towels. They looked to be about 16 or 17 years old. High school kids, but very shifty with their movements.

The gal was dressed in ripped jeans and Vans high tops; the dude was wearing a pair of jeans and his letterman jacket from West Rancho Niguel High School, a track and field athlete.

They still had on their sunglasses while they looked at the most expensive pots in the store, the Staub and the Le Creuset. Cast iron enameled pots called cocottes, made in France, with a price tag in the $400.00 range.

Maybe they were looking for a gift for their moms or dads. It seemed innocent, but I couldn't help my spidey sense that was going off like an alarm.

They circled the store, briefly checking out the Wusthof and the Miyabi Knives, with prices of $100.00 plus for them individually, and the block sets, at $800-$1200.00. They certainly had good taste in cooking products.

After a few minutes, they left.

I went back to searching through the towels and settled on some striped red and white from KAF, so durable and super cute in my kitchen. I also purchased some scented candles, one in the pine forest, one in peppermint twist, and one in orange clove, as well as matching soaps and lotions. These would be for the band gals.

I paid for my purchases and bid farewell!

"Thank you, Nikki. See ya next time."

"Bye, Joanne!"

I ran my gifts back home, put the gifts on the kitchen counter, and realized I hadn't purchased a Christmas tree for my own home.

The day had clouded up, and now it looked grey and cold outside! Tonight was girls' night out, and we were going to have drinks tonight, so my tree would have to wait a day.

It was already 3 pm, and I still needed to stop by Kendle's to do some paperwork. My phone chimed, "Rockin' Around the Christmas Tree."

"Hi, Matt,"

"Hi, darlin', I just wanted to apologize for this morning. Paul and I were out of line. We both said some dumb things, and I know that's why you left."

"Yeah, it was turning into a contest, and I hate that kind of stuff." I replied.

"I don't think he likes me very much; he probably feels threatened by me because we are good friends."

"Matt, you're a special friend, and I don't want to jeopardize that, so I think you should keep your distance."

"The last thing I want to do is upset you, so I will respect your wishes! Nikki, I'm not going to lie, I will always have a special place in my heart for you. I still love you, and I meant what I said last month, but I have to ask! Why *did* you break up with me? I know you mentioned that it had to do with the attention that you think I gain from other women, but I don't think that was entirely the reason!"

We were both quiet for a second; I knew he was waiting for me to tell him what had gone wrong. I wanted to tell him, and I did tell him.

What could I possibly say? I broke up with you because I was afraid of being dumped, but that wasn't the only reason!

Why did I continue to see him and even let him steal a few moments with me, a kiss, an embrace? Oh, yeah, that's right, because I'm still in love with him, but I'm dating someone else that I love too. That sounded selfish. Was I that far gone that I didn't have the courage to just make a commitment to one guy?

He spoke again,

" I just want you to know I'll be here for you."

He chose his words carefully, but that was Matt! The fire captain, the hero, the good guy, the Superman.

"You're right... I didn't give you the entire explanation, the truth, and I owe you that I ..."

In the background, I heard an alarm ring. He was at the station, and he was getting called to an emergency.

"We can talk later, I have to go." Then he hung up.

I got ready for my girls' night out this evening. I dressed in all black tonight. I put on my black Aurora Long Sleeve Lace Minidress with a sweetheart neckline by Bardot.

It was fabulous. I bought it last month, and I still haven't worn it.

I paired it with some black patent leather pumps, a red clutch purse, and red lipstick on my smackers. I grabbed my black leather jacket from the closet in case the temps dropped below 65 degrees tonight. I walked out to the bug and headed off to meet Roxi and Jessica at Blue 7.

I parked the bug in the public parking lot across from Coco Jo's. Her shop closed at 6 pm, and it was 8:30 pm, and the nightlife began around town.

I waved to Roxi and Jessica, and they were getting out of their cars as well.

"Hey guys, it's nice to see you both," I said, giving them quick hugs.

"Nikki, I love your dress, girl, that's gorgeous. Where do you find these things?"

"I'm a patient shopper, and I look for sales. You can always find some deals in the clearance section!"

"Come on, ladies, the first drink is on me!" Roxi chimed in.

We sat at a table in the corner. The place was busy, and we were lucky that Jessica's friend's boyfriend owned the place.

We had no wait time, and our table had a little reserved sign on it.

"Wow, Jessica, tell your friend thank you. We got in so fast, and look, we got the best table here, away from the crowds."

"I sure will." She answered.

Our server came and took our drink order, and we also ordered appetizers and our main dish. Blue Seven was one of the coolest places around town these days; the decor had a beach vibe.

A fancy resort style with modern touches, chic and high-end.

"This place reminds me of Newport Beach, guys. I have to say we are due for a girls' weekend there, spa days, beach days, and, of course, shopping!"

"Absolutely!" They both said.

I was looking around the restaurant, admiring the decor, when I saw the guy from the crime scene, the one who owns Rancho Arms and Tactical, the gun store.

He was talking to a server, and from the looks of it, he seemed to be having a heated discussion. The server said *no* by way of reading his lips and used a hand motion, saying no way!

The man who owned the gun and tactical store looked mad, he made a threat by waving his hand toward the server and then turned around and stormed out the door. The server looked around to see if anyone was looking his way.

At that moment, my eyes shifted to the bar, and he turned and walked to the kitchen. Strange, I wonder what that was about! I hadn't heard much about the case since this morning, and I knew Craig and Paul were investigating very intently and fast. I hope they catch whoever is behind the murder.

"Nikki, you zoned out again, girly."

"Oh, sorry about that. I was just thinking about yesterday's murder."

"Nikki, no more investigating, let's have some fun this evening!" Roxi stated.

"Ok, I'm turning it off, no more investigating. Let's go dance!"

We went to the dance floor and moved to the 90's night music.

"I'm just a girl." From No Doubt.

Our drinks arrived, and we went back to the table.

We raised our glasses of red wine, a raspberry mint mojito, and a dirty martini. "Waiting for Tonight" by JLo was playing! The night was just getting started.

"Cheers, ladies, here is to great friends."

"I'll drink to that!" Jessica replied.

Our appetizers of charcuterie arrived filled with meats, cheese, macron almonds, fig jam, chocolates, dried apricots, and honey.

After our dinner of salmon teriyaki, lemon chicken, and a dish of shrimp scampi, I had the salmon, of course.

We danced a few dances and then ordered nightcaps of Bailey's and coffee, and desserts.

We laughed and danced to a few Christmas songs, "All I Want for Christmas Is You" by Mariah Carey.

 We talked about guys, talked about work, and laughed some more until our dessert arrived.

I was laughing at Roxi's joke for Jessica; it was cute.

"Jessica, why do Dasher and Dancer love coffee?"

"I don't know why?" She replied.

"Because they're Santa's Starbucks!" Roxi finished the punch line.

We laughed not because of the joke so much, but just for the fact that we were having fun.

I happened to look at the bar and had to do a double-take.

Paul was sitting at the bar, having a drink with a pretty brunette.

I stopped laughing and tried to get a better look, but two girls were standing by the bar, blocking my view.

Roxi followed my gaze; she saw him, too, and then Jessica saw him.

No one said anything, so I changed the subject.

We finished our dessert, and when I casually looked to the bar again, he was gone, and so was she.

"Well, ladies, I think we should call it a night."

"Yes, I have a drumming for your soul class at the community center tomorrow at 9 am," Roxi commented.

We paid our bill and walked out of the restaurant. On our way to our cars, we noticed some blue and red lights flashing.

Joanne and her neighbor, Leslie Gray, who owned Lady Grays Tea Shoppe. The place everyone gets their tea from has lovely teapots and cups as well. Leslie Gray stood at 5'9, a former Physical fitness teacher. She kept in shape by hiking and running every morning. I had seen her a few times when I jogged around the mall, too.

She retired from the Rancho Niguel School District three years ago and then opened her dream store here on Main Street. The two women stood in front of their stores; the front windows smashed out on both businesses and glass was all over the sidewalk.

We jogged across the street, Jessica, Roxi, and I.

"Joanne, what happened? Are you all right?"

The uniformed officer taking notes turned to us and said,

"This is a crime scene, ladies; I need you to stand over there."

"Officer, these are friends of ours," Joanne said

"Ok!"

The officer replied.

"Oh, Nikki, this is terrible. Someone broke into our businesses and stole thousands of dollars in products!"

"She's right, Nikki, someone took thousands of dollars of merchandise from my store, too!" Leslie Gray stated.

"I'm so sorry to hear this. Do you have a suspect?"

I asked the officer.

"No, ma'am, we just arrived when the act was over."

He went back to writing something down, not even looking up when I was speaking.

Joanne's husband, Bob, stopped in front of the store. He had six wooden boards and a hammer to board up the windows out front.

Another uniformed officer came around from the back of the store, his flashlight in his hand.

"There's no sign of anyone back there anymore. Oh, hi Nikki!"

"Hello, Officer Ryan." I waved.

The officer taking Joanne and Leslie's information looked up at me

"I haven't had the pleasure yet; I'm Officer Yu. It's nice to finally meet thee, Nikki Rodriguez, wow, you're like a celebrity."

He smiled.

Officer Ryan spoke up again.

" She's Detective Anderson's girlfriend, too."

"I knew that." Officer Yu stated with a look that said Uh, duh.

The two young officers were very nice; they told Joanne and Leslie they would follow up and do some more patrols in the evening after closing time from here on out.

"Ok, we will follow up with you both in the coming week, please call us if you see some suspicious people or if you feel like something just doesn't sit right, please call us."

They left their business cards with them and headed out.

"Oh, Nikki, who would do this? Why, and so close to Christmas, people just don't have hearts anymore."

Joanne was sad now, and Leslie put her arm on her friend's shoulder.

"Don't worry, they will find the people responsible."

I tried to put her at ease.

Jessica reinforced my words.

"The police will find them. This happened a few years ago at my store, and it turned out to be some gang."

"They will catch them if I know the Rancho Niguel police,"
Roxi affirmed.

Joanne looked a little more reassured, she nodded her head yes to our comments, and thanked us for being so supportive.

After Bob boarded up both businesses and picked up the glass, we all went to our cars and headed home.

The street was now dark and lonely, with just a few street lights illuminating.

Chapter 6

You're Arresting Who?

I woke up at around 8:30 am the next morning; I turned on the local news channel five while still half asleep. I finished brushing my teeth and then showered, and just when I came out, I heard the story of the day.

"Police are looking for anyone who has information on a ring of thefts that occurred last night. Two stores in the Rancho Niguel mall, Coco Jo's and Lady Gray's Tea Shoppe, were burglarized, as well as a local gun store, Rancho Arms and Tactical. Thousands of dollars in merchandise were stolen, along with hundreds of dollars in damages. The three thefts occurred within a two-hour time frame. Police are looking at surveillance footage and Ring cams to find the perpetrators. If you have any information, please contact the Rancho Niguel police department at 555-1212. In other news, the governor of California has officially left his office after the recall vote passed last month. He will also be indicted on charges of money laundering, voter fraud, and misuse of state funds."

I got dressed and turned off the TV! I went to the kitchen to make coffee and breakfast. Halfway through my avocado toast, I got a call from Jessica.

"Nikki, get down to Dunner Art Gallery ASAP, the cops are there."

"What!" I asked, shocked.

"Just get down here!"

"Ok, I'm out the door!"

I grabbed my black riding boots, slipped them over my skinny jeans, grabbed my black leather jacket hanging in the front closet, and my keys, and rushed out.

I parked across the street in front of Pottery Barn in the 3-hour parking. I looked both ways and crossed the street! Three police cars and two black unmarked cruisers were parked in front.

I ran into the gallery to witness the search in progress. Cops in uniforms were taking boxes of stuff from the gallery, paintings had been removed from the walls, and the register and drawers under the counter were wide open and empty. Boxes were being taped up and labeled EVIDENCE. A woman in a navy pinstripe business suit was speaking with Paul and holding the warrant in her hands. Martin and Oliver were behind her. Oliver spotted me first

"Nikki, over here!"

He called to me, beckoning me over.

"What's going on?"

I asked him.

Complete dismay across his face.

Paul looked at me, silently apologetic, but returned to the lawyer he was speaking with.

Oliver pulled me aside and told me what was up.

"Nikki, you won't believe what has happened. We just got a warrant served this morning! They are searching the gallery for the stolen guns from Rancho Arms and Tactical. Can you believe that they got an anonymous tip that they were here? They have been looking all over the gallery; they turned the break room and our office upside down!"

Oliver was close to breaking down by this point.

"Detective Anderson, you'd better get down here." We then heard an officer say as he was coming up the stairs from the basement. "You need to see this detective!"

Paul and the lawyer followed the officer down the stairs, Martin, then Oliver, and I proceeded to go down the basement, too.

The basement was a daylight basement, a lower level that was more like a first floor rather than underground.

There was a large roll-down door and a single door at the back of the room where deliveries were brought in.

A large window brought in sunlight, but the shades were always drawn to protect any merchandise from outside view. The other side of the doors had an alley and three parking stalls for Martin and Oliver, and their staff.

Just behind a large metal shelf with sculptures on it sat a cardboard box on the floor covered with a blue blanket. The officer pulled off the blanket to reveal the stolen guns! Three semi-auto rifles with scopes on them from Geissele. A leader in manufacturing rifles, guns, and parts made in America, the box stated.

Martin put his hand to his mouth in amazement.

Oliver had to leave the room, and I was stunned!

Paul and the officer picked up the box with gloved hands and set it down on a workbench/counter a few feet away.

Paul called for the forensics team to come down. He turned to the lawyer and said.

"This changes everything!"

The lawyer turned to Martin, "Don't say a word, just let me do the talking."

Martin nodded, and he left the room to go upstairs. The lawyer then said to Paul, "I will be upstairs conversing with my clients in their office."

Paul nodded that he understood.

The CSI crew came downstairs with their tools and began to take prints.

Silently, I stood there like a statue with no words! I knew Martin and Oliver were innocent, but right now, seeing stolen merchandise in the basement of their art gallery, I knew they were being set up. By who? I had no idea, and why?

"Nikki, I need you to go upstairs. This is now a crime scene." Paul asked politely.

"Ok." That was all I could get out, and he followed me back up to the hallway.

"I know what you're thinking, and I'm going to tell you I don't believe that your friends did this. Just know that I'm on their side. This whole thing smells like a setup."

I nodded, still not saying anything.

"I don't want you to hate me right now because of what I have to do." He rubbed my arm.

"What!"

I said, now feeling clueless.

"Nikki, I'm going to have to arrest Martin and Oliver; they are in possession of stolen goods ."

"You're going to arrest who?"

"Nikki, did you hear what I told you? I have to arrest Martin and Oliver."

"No, you can't do this!" I objected with anger.

"It's my job, honey, but look, I'm going to find out what is going on, I know they are innocent, ok."

He reassured me.

"Yeah, I know," I said in a whisper.

"Maybe you shouldn't be here when I take them in."

"I'm going to bail them out. What are we looking at here?"

"First offense, stolen goods, no flight risk, I'd say about 5k each."

"Ok, I can do that!" I said, feeling my confidence come back.

"Are you ready?"

He looked into my eyes, asking me for support.

"Yeah, ok!"

He walked to Martin and Oliver's office and knocked on the door.

"Come in." The lawyer responded.

Paul walked in, and I followed.

"Martin, Oliver, I hate to have to do this, but I'm going to need you two to come with me to the station. I won't cuff you, but I need to take you in the cruiser."

"We understand," Martin responded.

"I will bail you two out immediately!" I stated.

"We don't want you to go to the trouble, Nikki. We have the money for it, our lawyer can handle everything."

Oliver replied, reassuring me they had it all taken care of.

"I'm so sorry, guys, I feel terrible."

"We know you're on our side, Nikki. We will get through this!"

Martin told me.

"It's time to go," Paul said, leading them out the door.

I walked behind their lawyer.

"If you need more money, please call me," I told her, handing her my business card from Kendle's as owner and operator.

"Thank you, Nikki."

She said, taking my card and tucking it in her purse.

"They will be out by this evening, don't worry."

"Thank you,"

I replied, feeling relieved.

Paul led Martin and Oliver to the cruiser; a few passers-by had now gathered, wondering what was going on.

Down the street, I saw a news van and a reporter heading over.

Paul put them in the car right away and drove off before the press descended upon them.

The lawyer headed off, and so did I.

There wasn't much I could do right now, but one thing was for sure: I needed to clear Martin and Oliver's names.

I'm sure this will be in the news, and I didn't want their reputation trashed. I had to find out who was doing this to my friends and why.

Chapter 7

Surfs Up

After I left the art gallery, I couldn't think of what my next move would be. I was angry, frustrated, and just in a bad mood. So when I'm stressed, or I need to regroup and get my head on, I go to my happy place.

I stopped by the condo, put on my swimsuit and a pair of shorts, grabbed my wetsuit and my surfboard from the garage, and drove to Newport Beach.

The day was fair with a high of 73 and sunny, perfect December weather, not a cloud in sight, and not a snowflake to be physically found!

I had the beach to myself; there were a few other beachcombers and about maybe three dudes catching some bitchin waves.

Other than that, it was sparse and, for a weekday, wasn't unusual.

I had to have the top down to fit my board, and luckily, I kept a Dodger cap and hair ties in my car.

I pulled some SPF from the glove compartment and put it on my face. When I arrived, I parked in the lot, free during the week, and then I pulled on my wetsuit, the one Paul had given me last summer. I then grabbed my beach bag and board and headed to the sand.

I took my beach blanket out of my bag, set it down, and dropped my bag on there. I put my driver's license and a credit card in my wetsuit pocket on the inside of my suit. I had locked up my phone in the car; I placed my keys in a plastic bag with my sunglasses and lip balm. I rolled the items in my towel and put my old college sweatshirt on top of it. I grabbed my board and went in.

On my first two rides, I wiped out; I wasn't focusing.

It had been a few weeks since I had been out on the water. Paul and I drove out here to Newport Beach, then, and we had a great time. It was right before Thanksgiving when we left to see his family at his parents' house in Lake Havasu.

We started early, I practiced my stance and caught my first barrel, or better said, a hollow wave when it breaks. It was the end of all that most surfers live for. He had promised me we would go somewhere special for a mini vacation and find some new surfing beaches.

Today, my third wave, a much better one, I caught a party wave (A wave surfed by several people at once). I rode in with the three other dudes who were here when I arrived.

It was awesome, and I came up with my first clue to look for. I was going to call Roxi and see if she wanted to go with me to Rancho Gun and Tactical.

I need to see the store owner for myself and see what kind of vibe he gives off. Tomorrow would be a better day for going to do some investigating.

"Hey, guys, looks like we have a Betty."

One of the dudes said when we came to shore.

"You're pretty good. How long have you been surfing?"

Another dude asked.

"Just since last summer," I responded.

"Cool!" Another one of them replied.

"Just watch out, we saw a few grey suits out there, one of them came close."

"Thanks."

They gave me a hang-loose and went back in.

My surf lingo had improved, and I knew what they meant.

A Betty- a gal who surfs.

A grey suit - a shark.

I thought of going back in, but I was hungry, I packed it up, got in the bug, and headed to the nearest In-N-Out Burger.

A double-double and fries had my name on them!

The cool ocean air blew by me; I sat at a table outside, eating my burger.

The drive-thru was loaded with cars, and inside, the booths were full. I thought about the thieves who would steal from Coco Jo's and Lady Gray's Tea shoppe, *and* the Gun shop all in one night? They only found the stolen guns in Martin and Oliver's shop. What about the items from the other two stores? Why didn't they find the other items at the gallery?

Why only stash the guns but not the other items? The answer is: They only wanted the guns found! There were two separate thefts, two were connected, and one was not!

By the time I finished my burger and fries, I knew that the two thefts at Coco Jo's and Lady Grays from the night before were connected; they were burglarized by the same people! The gun theft was different! It was like the other two thefts were a distraction or a useful occurrence to justify why the gun theft was done! I couldn't put my finger on it.

I wanted to call Paul and tell him my theory, but I knew that he would want to know why I was meddling again.

Well, the answer was simple: someone was trying to hurt my friends, and I wasn't going to let that happen!

I got back in the bug, I turned on the radio to the Pandora music app, and Christmas classics came on. "Feliz Navidad" by Jose Feliciano

I sang along, thinking of my next strategy to find a clue to help clear Martin and Oliver's names. Once again, I had to go sleuthing, and even if it was behind Paul's back, I had good cause.

Chapter 8

A Hunting I Will Go

Last night, I called Roxi and asked her to come with me to Rancho Arms and Tactical.

"Girl, heck yeah, let's go shake this guy down."

"We are just going to observe right now, maybe ask a few questions. We can't let him know that we are investigating him."

"Wait, what are we going to say?"

"We are going to go and buy a gun!"

I told Roxi to come by my place at 10 am, and then we would go in my car.

It was late last night when I got a call from Martin.

He and Oliver had bailed out; it was less than they had thought, $3k each, and they had to surrender their passports.

Martin said that Paul was able to put them in a cell by themselves, the nicest one they had, and that their lawyer was impressed with the department. They also said that when they were released, Matt was there to pick them up and take them to dinner.

"You guys didn't call me!"

"We're sorry it was last-minute."

"I'm just glad you guys are out."

"So are we, Nikki! At least they didn't charge us with murder! Those guns had no prints on them, so we don't know who handled them or why they were in our basement! Why is someone doing this to us?"

"Martin, I'm going to find out!"

***

I came back to the present; I looked at the weather app on my phone,

Rancho Niguel

> *high 59*
>
> *low 42*

A cold front is moving into the area,
The lowlands and mountains will see lows
in the 30s, valleys, and inland will
See lows in the 40s
Beaches will have a high of 65
with a low of 50

The weather was changing; storms were coming in.

I opted for dark jeans and a red sweater.

My doorbell rang; it was Roxi.

"Roxi, here reporting for duty!"

She came in dressed in all black, her platinum blond hair in a black baseball cap, too!

"We *are* going in through the front door."

I chuckled.

"I know!" she said confidently.

"Let's *go*!"

I turned the brim of her hat sideways and giggled.

We arrived at the gun shop, parked the bug, and went in.

I was surprised by how modern and sleek this place was.

Walking in, I expected heads on the wall, green carpet, and cigars. To my surprise, this place was decked out with dark hardwood floors, glass display counters, and rifles! Semi-autos hung on a wall behind the counter, illuminated by blue neon lighting. Black leather sleek seating, a bar counter with a blue lighted fridge, with soft drinks and mineral waters.

High-end gear, holsters, bags, targets, and tactical flashlights were displayed on modern floating wood shelves. A large black staircase led to an upstairs range, I assumed. I heard gunshots that sounded like light thumps. Some men with ear protection muffs, carrying a gun box, were coming downstairs with targets they shot.

A few customers browsed around, two people were waiting at the front counter, and one woman was being helped by an employee. Roxi and I walked up to the counter and glanced over the selections. I spotted Glocks, Sig Sauers, H&K, Walther, Springfield Armory, Kimber, Beretta, S&W, and Wilson Combat, just to name a few.

High-end handguns, 1911, P238, 45s, and so forth.

Some guns were in stainless steel, black, tan, mossy green, Tiffany blue, and even pink.

"May I help you two ladies?"

An older man in black jeans and a black Glock long-sleeve T-shirt asked us from behind the counter. I had recognized him as the man who spoke to Paul in the parking lot when the body was found. He was the owner of Rancho Guns and Tactical. He was also the guy who was arguing with the server at Blue 7.

I didn't know what we were here to look at, but I made up a story quickly.

"Um, yes, my friend here wants to buy a gun, and we were told this is the place to shop."

"Of Course, we have an excellent selection for women, the best guns are here."

He replied. Did I detect a slight Russian accent?

Roxi gave me a look of fear, her eyes wide, and crept out.

I gave her a reassuring look.

"My friend is a little apprehensive about guns; I think she's afraid of them. But I'm helping her to see they are easy to handle and can save your life."

I smiled.

He bought it hook, line, and sinker. He smiled and proceeded to show us some guns from the glass case.

"I like that Tiffany Blue gun right there!" Roxi pointed out.

"Glock 19 gen 4, that's a very good gun."

He opened the glass case and showed Roxi the gun sights, the safety, and how to rack back the slide.

I casually asked him.

"Was this the same store that was robbed a few days ago?"

He stopped what he was telling Roxi and stated.

"Yes, it was unfortunate; we were robbed, but we did get our merchandise back. A crazy world we live in."

He grimaced; he smelled like menthol cigarettes.

"I agree!"

I replied.

Roxi held the gun in her hand, and the owner behind the counter,

helping us, whose name tag read Vic, demonstrated how to hold

the gun and what your posture should look like.

How your grip and stance should be, too.

"You two should take my women's only class, beginning firearms

for the ladies."

I nodded.

 "I think we should sign up for that, right, Roxi?"

She turned and gave me a look of no. I once again pleaded with her

with my look of Come on, just say yes.

"Uh, yeah, that would be fun."

She finally responded with a smile.

"Ok, I will get the forms, and the class is $40.00 each, and we

supply the guns and the training, and you get to shoot at our

range."

"You have a range here?"

I asked.

"Yes, upstairs, I will show you."

He pointed to the large staircase, and then

he went off to search for the forms from an office shelf behind

him.

"Nikki, I don't want to go to a gun class."

She whispered.

"You don't have to; we can cancel it. I'm just getting a feel of this place. I think he seems kinda sketchy, what do you think?"

"Yeah, he seems like the type that will get upset if you say no to him, that's what I'm reading !"

Another employee was ringing up some holsters for a customer; he was young, with a permanent scowl on his face! I figured maybe he was in his early 20s; he wore a black T-shirt with the words Geissele on the front written in white lettering.

I only noticed him because his tattoo was really interesting. It caught my eye; it was a lady in red!

We filled out our forms, I paid the $80.00, and we were due to come back tomorrow at 2 pm.

He took us upstairs to see a state-of-the-art range, all automated targets moved back and forth, stations illuminated with neon blue lights, and a range master stood there at all times for any questions and to ensure safety was being the priority.

 "Safety first always is what we promote,"

Vic told us after the tour, and then we went back downstairs.

Roxi was looking a bit overwhelmed.

I had looked around the shop, and everything seemed to be in order. The owner seemed like a guy who was polite but could become a firestorm if provoked.

"Thank you for all of your help!"

I said as we were leaving.

"See you tomorrow!" Roxi chimed in.

We opened the door and walked out, but not before I noticed the young employee with the scowl walk over and whisper something to Vic, and it sent a chill down my spine!

Chapter 9

Information Please

After leaving the Rancho Arms and Tactical store, Roxi and I went to get some lunch. The clouds moved in, and heavy rain came down. Of course, when it rains, we Californians lose our minds, we act like it's going to hurt us, water, raindrops, can you imagine? Everyone gets unglued, umbrellas are everywhere, and car accidents are in abundance.

On our way to Kendle's, we had some stop-and-go traffic, a blue Camry, and a Black BMW hit! An ambulance and a fire truck were on the scene.

While driving by, I came to a stop, rolled my window down, and Roxi and I waved to Matt. His team was on the scene, along with Anita and James, my friends, and the paramedics.

"Hi Matt, is everyone ok?"

"Hey, darlin' and Roxi!"

He smiled brightly.

"Hi, Matt!" Roxi responded.

"This one wasn't too bad, a broken leg, and the other guy might have a concussion. Medics are going to take both of them to the hospital. I think they were lucky, I've seen much, much worse!"

"I'm sure you've seen a lot! By the way, just a reminder: don't forget about the community center Christmas Fest tonight. Roxi and I will be caroling with a group of friends."

"I will be there. The station has a booth, and we are taking donations for the annual Toys for Tots."

Our attention was diverted by many cars beginning to honk their horns in support of the now-famous Santa Streaker! He ran along the sidewalk, yelling, "**MERRY CHRISTMAS, EVERYONE!**"

A few people on the street cheered him on, whistling and clapping for him! The police on the scene just shook their heads. They didn't pursue him. What was the point? For some strange reason, they couldn't catch him!

Roxi and I chuckled, Matt laughed and remarked, "Oh boy."

"**MERRY CHRISTMAS, RANCHO NIGUEL**!" The streaker yelled again, now running off toward the park and green belt across the street.

We were now being told to move along, the traffic officers waving us by.

"We'll see you there." Roxi chimed.

"See ya, Matt," I said.

"Later, Darlin, drive safe!" He winked.

Roxi smiled as I rolled the window up.

"Oh my gosh, that man still has it bad for you, he still looks at you like he adores you!"

She smiled with a flirtatious grin.

"We're just friends, Roxi, we both agreed."

I tried to reassure her, but I knew she wasn't buying it!

"Roxi's not getting involved, just saying!"

She sat back in her seat and checked her phone for messages.

We arrived at Kendle's; lunch was slow today, I guess just a few people were dining, and three customers were at the bar.

"Hi Tito, how's it going?"

"Oh, not too bad, ladies. We had a lunch rush an hour ago, but now it seems like everyone went back to Christmas shopping."

Daisy came into the dining room.

"Hi Nikki, Hi Roxi."

"Hi, Daisy!" Roxi and I said in unison.

"There was a car accident down the street, and the Santa Streaker was out again," Roxi told Daisy and Tito.

"Not again, man, that guy is tenacious, and you guys know when it rains, people drive recklessly," Tito replied.

"This one wasn't that bad, light injuries, thank God!"

I piped in.

"Good to hear it wasn't serious, but about that Santa Streaker, why can't they catch him?" Asked Daisy.

"That's the same question I'm asking," I replied.

"Can I get you both any lunch?"

Daisy asked us.

"Oh yeah, I'll take a Chicken Parmesan with extra garlic bread and a glass of Red,"

Roxi said, putting in her order.

"What about you, Nikki?"

"I think a club sandwich and a cup of tomato soup, and to drink, I'll take some hot tea, it's getting cold out there."

"Coming right up."

She smiled and went back to the kitchen.

"Nikki, Paul came by earlier, and he asked me to give this to you."

Tito handed me a note.

"Oh, thanks, did he stay for lunch?"

"Yeah!"

Tito was short and quick with his response.

" I wonder why he didn't call me."

"He said it was a business lunch, somebody from the mayor's office,"

Tito replied as he was cleaning the bar, wiping a white bar mop over the counter.

Right away, my mind went to Stacie, Paul's old girlfriend from LA, who had recently moved here. She's the new mayor's assistant. This is the third time he has been dining with her.

"Was it Stacie?"

"All he told me was someone from the mayor's office!"

"Thanks, Tito,"

I said, feeling like I had been punched in the gut.

Tito saw this, too!

He gave me a comforting smile.

I opened the note, which was folded into a small square. Roxi answered a call that came in on her phone, and Tito went to make our drinks.

Paul's note read:

Hey, Sunshine, you're probably wondering why I'm writing a note. I was sort of conned into coming to lunch with Stacie; it's nothing romantic; it has to do with police department business, but I want to be transparent with you, which is why I came here. Your staff is

beyond loyal to you, and I wanted to be out in the open so
everyone could see this was just business, not a date, not an
opportunity for her to come between us. So I'll call you tonight. I
can come by with some late-night snacks. Text me.
Paul.

I felt a smile come to my mouth; I was now feeling very guilty for thinking the worst. I had to trust him.

I had to let go of my fears of relationships and cheating. I had to give this a chance and not run away as I did before. I folded the note and tucked it in my purse.

After having lunch with Roxi, she left to go shopping with her boyfriend. I went upstairs to brainstorm all of the clues I had so far.

Clues:

1.) 3 thefts, two related and one not related.

2.) Merchandise from only one of the robberies was found.

3.) The locations of one of the robberies were too far apart from the others.

4.) One of the shops had an employee who turned up dead.

5.) One of the robberies was at the convention at the Huntington Hotel/where a body was found.

6.) All of the clues lead to Rancho Arms and Tactical.

Questions:

1.) What is the connection between Martin and Oliver and their art gallery?

2.) Who has access to the art gallery?

3.) Why was the art gallery used?

4.) How did the thieves gain access to the gallery?

5.) Who is Ivan Smirnov?

6.) What does the waiter at Blue 7 have to do with Vic Parker, the owner of Rancho Arms and Tactical?

After writing this all out, I had to have some answers. I decided to go to Blue 7 and try to speak to the waiter there and find out what the beef was between him and Vic!

I locked up the office and let Daisy know I was going out for a while and that I would meet her and Tito tonight for Caroling.

"Ok, I'll see you tonight, Nikki,"

Daisy called out as I went out the door.

I zipped up my red raincoat and headed to Blue 7.

It was around 4 pm, and most of the customers in Blue 7 were having drinks, and a few happy hour appetizers were coming out of the kitchen.

I went in and sat at the bar.

"Can I get you anything to drink?"

A young bartender came to take my order.

"Sure, how about an Irish coffee!"

"Coming right up!"

I searched the restaurant for the server; I saw a few cocktail servers and one female server, but not the dude from the other night.

"Here you are."

"Thank you!"

I accepted my drink.

The bartender went down the way to take another customer's order. I took a long sip and searched once again for the server. Finally, he came out of the kitchen with a large platter of artichoke dip and bread; he set it down at a table of three ladies with tropical drinks.

He made his way to the bar just a foot away from me.

"Hey, Bry, can I get three more sunset beaches for table 23?"

He asked the young bartender whose name tag read Bryan.

"Sure!"

He replied and went to work making those drinks.

At that moment, I took a chance and just introduced myself.

"The drinks here are wonderful."

"Yeah, you can say that."

The server responded.

I tried to go in for a more detailed conversation.

I didn't know how to start it, but I just came out with it.

"I saw you a few days ago, you were speaking with that man named Vic, the owner of Rancho Guns and Tactical!"

His eyes narrowed as if he was wondering what I was trying to find out.

"What's it to you?"

He said, irritation nagging in his voice.

"He looked pretty upset with you. Are you ok?"

"Maybe you should just mind your own business."

He stated angrily with contempt.

"Does it have anything to do with the robberies?"

I blurted out with desperation.

"You're a beautiful woman, if you want to stay that way, mind your own business!"

With that, he grabbed his drinks and left.

Ok, that didn't go very well.

The color on my face now became a shade paler!

"Don't mind Jack; he's just on edge because he's losing his house."

The bartender stated after hearing some of the brush-off from the server.

"Oh, that's terrible!" I exclaimed.

"Yeah, it's his fault. The dude is a gambler, and now he basically begs the owner for more hours to work. I guess he had some big deal cooking last week, but it fell through!

Now, he barks at everyone who looks at him the wrong way. I'd like to say I feel bad for the guy, but he hangs out with the red mafia and bad gamblers!"

"Red mafia?"

I managed to say.

"Yeah, you know some cosmonauts, Russians!"

"Oh yeah! I know what you mean."

I replied.

"Real shady characters!"

"You mean like the guy who owns Rancho Arms and Tactical?"

I mentioned to him that maybe he knew what the argument was about. Maybe he knew Vic!

"Oh, you mean Vic! That guy does rub me the wrong way; he was here a few days ago talking to Jack. I guess Jack used to work at his store and gave him a loan. Remember, I said gambling!"

He gave me the wink, wink look to indicate the taboo topic that Jack was involved in.

So Jack took out a loan from Vic, that's very interesting!

"So just between you and me, Jack is an all right guy, I guess, but Vic, that guy's trouble! Jack came into the bar one day, and it slipped that he owed Vic a big-time favor. He told me if he didn't follow through on this, Vic would never let it go."

My eyes shot up!

The bartender nodded to show his enthusiasm about what he was telling me.

A gal a few seats down called him and asked for a Crantini.

"Gotta go, work calls!"

"Hey, thanks for the info."

"Anytime."

Wow! Was he filled with a lot of information, and why did he tell me all of this? I always thought bar tenders were the ones who were *the* listeners. Well, I guess he did listen to what everyone else *was* saying!

I got up, finished the rest of my drink, and left two twenties on the bar!

I put my raincoat back on and went out into the storm!

Chapter 10

Caroling, Caroling, We Go

What came to my mind first was the thought: What was Vic asking Jack to do?

I parked the car and ran inside before more rain came pounding down. I put on the tea kettle and grabbed a red cup and a tin box of peppermint twist tea.

I hung my raincoat in the shower and took off my wet socks that were soaked.

I put my athletic socks on the hearth and turned on the fireplace.

I found my fleece-lined moccasins in front of the sofa and settled in.

I wrapped my ivory afghan around me until the chill went away.

I sent Paul a text asking him how the case was going.

He responded with a sad face emoji, and not good!

I had to find another opportunity to talk to Jack, the server, over at Blue 7; he knows something.

Maybe I should tell Paul what I saw, and then he can speak to Jack.

I sent another text to Paul.

> *"I have to tell you, a few nights ago*
> *I was out with Roxi and Jessica at Blue 7.*
> *I saw a server, Jack, that's what his name tag said, arguing with*
> *that guy from the crime scene on the day of Diaz's wedding!*
> *The one who owns Rancho Tactical. He looked pretty upset, and the*
> *the server was saying no way to him, and then he stormed out!*
> *They were both very angry. Do you think it means anything?"*

I waited a few minutes for him to get back to me. The tea kettle whistled, and I made my tea, took it back to the couch, and curled up again in my afghan. He then responded with:

> *"Thanks for the tip, I'm going to check it out!"*
> *"I'll see you later tonight at the Community Center."*

I felt like maybe I was getting somewhere! Now, if I couldn't get Jack to talk, then maybe Paul could.

I also decided to call Martin and Oliver.

It rang twice, and then Oliver answered.

"Hi, Nikki!"

"Hi, how are you both holding up?"

"Oh, Nikki, it's been just awful. The gallery is still closed, and Martin and I don't know when we can open back up. They did say we can open if we want to, but we feel like we need to at least wait until we can get a cleaning crew in there.

97

We have a big mess! Merchandise, fingerprint dust, papers, trash, uh, it's a nightmare!"

"Well, let me tell you what I have so far."

Oliver put me on speakerphone, and I gave Matin and Oliver the rundown on what I had.

I gave them my theory on the robberies, the owner, Vic, and the server at Blue 7, and the information about what they found at the victim Ivan's home. I also mentioned the guns that were sent to the gallery by mistake when they were having trouble with the shipping company.

"Do you think those deliveries have something more to do with what happened?" I asked.

"We thought about that too, and we told Paul, and he said he is looking into everything. Nikki, we want to thank you for investigating. We appreciate it, but Oliver and I don't want you to put yourself in the crosshairs of a killer."

I could tell they were genuinely worried about me from the sound of their pleas.

"I have been very discreet; no one is on to me. I need to help you two; I know someone is setting you both up!"

"Our lawyer has been very positive about our non-involvement; she thinks that this case will be wrapped up soon, and we will be cleared of any wrongdoing."

"That's good to hear, guys. Paul knows it's a setup, too, but *why* and *who* is what we need to find out."

"Nikki, promise me you will let Paul handle the big stuff. Honey, he's a professional."

"I have been giving Paul some leads to look into, trust me, the last thing I want is to come face to face with a killer!"

After my call with Martin and Oliver, I finished my tea and fell asleep for a two-hour nap.

When I woke up, it was already dark outside. I had an hour and a half before I had to be at the community center. I looked at my weather app again, and it read:

Clear and cold

A high of 42 degrees

I decided to dress warmly,

I put on a pair of flannel-lined jeans and a warm cream-colored sweater with a waffle Henley under it in the same color.

My LL Bean purchases were going to pay off now. I grabbed an emerald green crocheted scarf and my red wool coat that covered my bum and went down to my mid-thigh.

I added a red beret and some cream-colored gloves. Ok, I was festive and ready to go! I grabbed my keys, put my wallet and phone in my jacket pocket, and was on my way!

Despite the cold, I walked across the street to the community center; there was no point in driving, I knew Paul would drive me back.

The community center was warm and toasty, and the large room held tables with different businesses selling last-minute gift items, crafts, candles, candies, jams, and gift baskets filled with cookies, popcorn, coffee, and other novelty items.

A large Christmas tree in the center of the room was decorated with multi-colored lights and glass ornaments in many novelty colors and themes: baseballs, skates, Santa, boats, canoes, log cabins, pancakes, an avocado, a spaceship, a stand mixer, golf clubs, palm trees, boots, you name it, it was on the tree. These beautiful ornaments were made by Old World Christmas, located in Spokane, Washington. The spectacular PNW, I'll have to get up there one of these days.

I met up with my fellow carolers at the community choir booth. We had a large turnout this year. Fifteen of my fellow Rancho Niguel residents gathered around, the cups of coffee and peppermint hot chocolate being passed around by Jessica.

"Everyone, warm up, get some coffee and hot chocolate. It's cold outside, and we will be covering four blocks!"

Jessica shouted.

Starbucks proudly donated free beverages to the carolers. They also had a booth right next to ours, selling fresh coffee, lattes, mochas, hot chocolates, and gifts.

Everyone was in good spirits, and it seemed nice to have Christmas cheer during this time.

Mrs. Green and Marge were here with their plus ones, Betty Jean from the real estate office and her date, Roxi, Tito and Daisy, Craig and Kiana, Sonya and her husband Charlie, and of course, me. I counted everyone off, all here except Paul, and I guessed that maybe his investigation once again prevented him from having some free time.

"I'm ready to go caroling,"

Matt said, coming up to our group.

"You're going to come caroling with us? You don't know the songs."

"Roxi gave me a copy of the music last week; I've been rehearsing all week."

He smiled.

I gave Roxi a look that said. What did you do behind my back?

She smiled and walked away.

"Ok, the more the merrier, let's go."

I surrendered.

Matt was dressed for caroling; he donned black jeans and a grey wool sweater under his black wool peacoat. He had a red scarf around his neck and black leather gloves; he even had on the right shoes, a pair of black Danner Super Rainforest GTX boots.
He added his favorite beanie, in red and grey with a moose on it, from the movie Home Alone. Yup, the kind Macaulay Culkin wore in the movie. I have one at home, too! Just something we bought together at Outdoor World a few years ago.

"If everyone is ready, let's go!"

We gathered around the Christmas tree, now everyone holding their brown choral leather books with our music. We were just about to begin when Ms. Mayor CJ Groves walked up to us with a tall brunette in a red sweater dress and long dark hair.

"I just wanted to let you all know that we are so happy to have you caroling in the neighborhoods this evening. There is nothing more traditional and uniting than being a part of your community."
She smiled a plastic politician's grin, shook our hands, and then again thanked us.

The tall brunette kept her attention on me the whole time. I had to introduce myself to break the glare she cast on me.

"I don't believe I've had the pleasure; I'm Nikki Rodriguez!" I finally said.

She extended her hand to me and replied,

"I'm Stacie Mc. Daniels, the mayor's Executive Assistant."

Her handshake was minimal, like when people really don't want to touch your hand because maybe they are appalled to have to.

She didn't smile, just kept a resting bitch face, not friendly or warm, just like an evil statue of cold beauty.

She turned her attention to Matt next, a full smile coming to her cherry red lips, her dark eyes shining bright.

"It's nice to see you again, Captain Stevens."

Matt shook her hand and replied, "Likewise."

He smiled.

I wanted to puke!

Stacie Mc. Daniels was going to be trouble for me!

We began our first song. "It's beginning to look a lot like Christmas," and then we sang our next song while walking out of the community center into the cold night air, "Let it snow."

We walked down the street to the first homes by the town center.

A few people came outside to see us. They held their phone lights up in the air. We held flameless candles for light, and two of us had a mini-mag flashlight as a backup.

We came upon St. Mark's Catholic Church, where a small crowd had just finished mass. We sang "The First Noel."

When we were done, we received applause, and Father Riley blessed us.

We walked on and sang our next song, "Jingle Bell Rock," at the park that had been transformed into an outdoor ice skating rink. We got such an outpouring from the audience that we did two more songs there.

"It's The Most Wonderful Time of The Year" and "Winter Wonderland."

After that, we walked back toward the mall and Community Center, singing "O Holy Night."

We stopped in front of the Community Center and Library and wrapped up our last song in the Children's Garden. We finished with a fun and fast "12 Days of Christmas."

We were chilly, with red noses and rosy cheeks, but we all put our arms around each other and sang like a chorus line, but not kicking up our frozen legs. We had a large crowd of shoppers that joined us, and soon we were all singing.

When we were done, everyone clapped and cheered, and a few whistles and woo-hoos from people in the mall. We had smiles from ear to ear, we laughed and hugged one another.

"Thank you, everyone, for joining me this evening. You are all so dear to my heart," I told our group.

"This was a blast," Craig replied.

"We are doing this again next year!" Mrs. Green chimed in

I had the same comments from everyone else, too!

"This was so much fun!"

"We had such a cool time."

"Let's do this every year!"

Then we heard it...

"**MERRY CHRISTMAS, EVERYONE**!" the Santa Streaker smiled and ran by.

Chapter 11

Not another One!

After the Santa Streaker struck again, we all went back inside the Community Center. Everyone went off to get more coffee to warm up at the Starbucks booth. Some went to purchase items at other booths.

Matt, Roxi, and I went to the fireplace to warm up.

"That guy is crazy!" Roxi blurted out.

"He is getting everyone's attention; maybe he's the Christmas angel, spreading holiday cheer."

Matt said, making a joke.

I just rolled my eyes.

I scanned the room casually and saw Paul coming into the front entry. I waved to him and smiled. On his way over to us, Stacie stopped him and led him over to the mayor. Paul gave an apologetic smile, and the mayor shook his hand as they engaged in conversation.

Roxi noticed this too, and she gave me a sympathetic look. She leaned over and whispered.

"I don't trust that Stacie."

"I know!" I replied.

Paul now made his way over to us.

"Hi, Roxi, Matt!"

The guys acknowledged each other with nods and barely looked at one another.

"Matt, can I buy you a hot chocolate?" Roxi asked him.

Matt took the hint and graciously accepted her offer.

"Of course, thank you. Nikki, I just want to say the caroling was more than I expected. I'm looking forward to next year."

With that, he and Roxi headed over to the Starbucks booth.

I waved.

"I'm sorry I missed it!" Paul said, looking apologetically at me.

"I went and interviewed that guy, Jack, and you were right. Get this! He told me that the guy, Vic, has a history of shady loans that he gives out to people.

He said he took a small loan from him, and he paid it back with a 10% interest, but the guy won't leave him alone; he keeps asking for a favor."

"What kind of favor?" I asked.

"Making some deliveries, he said that Vic never gave him specifics, but that he needed a driver to deliver some goods off to Long Beach Port. The thing is that we don't know what he wanted to be delivered, and there's nothing illegal about asking someone for a favor; we don't know what he wanted to be moved."

"So you can't question him about it?"

"We can ask him about it, but there's no point! He can lie to us, and we have no way of proving he was doing anything wrong. He can say he was moving items of furniture or products from his store, nothing illegal. The only thing we *can* do is stake out his place to see if he *is* doing something illegal."

"So there's nothing?"

Paul was thinking about what I just asked, and then he said,

"Come to think of it, we have a connection!"

Paul said, having an a-ha moment.

"You know, Vic told us that he gave Ivan, his employee who was killed, a loan too.

Remember when you said Craig told you about the money we found at Ivan's home? Well, according to Vic, he said Ivan needed the money for some family emergency."

"This guy, Vic, seems to have a history of giving out loans to people who work for him, coincidence or not?"

I asked Paul.

"It's worth looking into."

Paul and I were hungry, and we decided to go to get some cheeseburgers from the Lou's Diner booth that was next to the Starbucks booth.

Paul ordered a beer and a Ronald Regan Cowboy burger, 100% beef, cheddar cheese, BBQ sauce, tomato, lettuce, bacon, and fried onion straws.

I opted for a Roy Rogers beverage and a "How to Marry a Millionaire" grease burger, 100% beef, cheddar cheese, shredded lettuce, tomato, pickles, and 1000 island dressing.

We shared an order of shoestring fries and Ketchup. Paul and I found some seats away from the crowd and had a moment to relax.

"So I had a chance to meet Stacie." I calmly told him.

"Oh, that's nice!" He said it as more of a casual approval.

"I don't think she likes me,"

I told him, gauging his response.

"She has been asking me to be a part of this new outreach program for youth mentoring. I told her I would think about it. I'm busy with all of my cases, but she said it would be a big push for her career because the mayor wants to get this community involved with preventing school violence.

It's a good program. Stacie has always been a big supporter of kids and schools; it means a lot to her."

"It does sound like a good program; you should do it."

I took a bite of my burger to keep myself from asking him why Stacie's career was *so* important to him.

"Nikki! Don't worry about Stacie, I like you, and that's all that matters."

He looked at me with those beautiful sea-green eyes.

I asked him.

"By the way, do you have a Christmas Angel?"

"Not yet!"

"Oh *really!*"

"I haven't had time, but the biggest donation gets extra vacation time."He smiled with an arch of his eyebrow.

"Yes, I've heard! Craig told me that you were already spoken for and conned me into being his Christmas Angel!"

Paul cracked up!

"Oh my gosh, Craig is off the charts! Man, is he competitive."

"I just happen to have an idea, so how about we do this!"

I made a plan for Paul to have that vacation time in the bag!

We were having fun shopping at all of the booths. Paul purchased some gift baskets for his siblings and a nice afghan made from wool in a beautiful ocean blue for his mom to go with the new chaise he bought her.

She loves to read mystery novels by the window, looking out at the lake. It's one of her favorite pastimes.

I bought a few jams of Huckleberry and Appleberry.

Plus, two throw blankets, one in cream and one in heather grey, last-minute gifts I had forgotten about.

It was just about 7:45 pm, and we were ready to head home when Paul got a call.

"This is Detective Anderson."

He answered.

His good mood changed, and now he was upset.

"When?"

"Ok," I'll be right there!"

He hung up his phone and turned to me

"Jack is dead!"

"Not another one!"

Chapter 12

The lady in Red

Paul and I drove over to the crime scene, where Jack was found. The police closed off the street about a block down from Blue 7. Red and blue lights flashed, yellow crime scene tape was already put up, and Detective Sonya Smith and Craig were already interviewing witnesses.

They had gotten there faster than we did. After our caroling, Craig, Kiana, Sonya, and her husband, Charlie, had just gotten to a restaurant across the street when it happened.

We walked past the police tape; Paul went directly to Sonya. "So, what happened?"

"Let's just say it's not what you wanted to hear. He took two bullets to the chest."

Craig walked up to us, "Witnesses said that he was crossing the street from his car parked over there."

Sonya and Craig pointed to a black Kia.

"A dark vehicle came around the corner, and a suspect wearing black gloves, dark glasses, and a black baseball cap shot him. Then sped away!"

"A black baseball cap, dark glasses, and a black car that narrows it down," Paul replied, irritated!

"One of the witnesses said the cap he was wearing had white lettering, and the last couple of letters were ERS!"

Craig read from his little notebook.

Then it hit me: I knew that ball cap, I had seen it once before!

"I know what the cap said!

Rancho Raiders, the mascot of Cal State Rancho Niguel. The night of Diaz's wedding, I was on my way to the ladies' room, and I saw two guys talking. One guy had the same ball cap, and he turned the other way when I walked by as if he didn't want to be noticed by anyone. I thought it was strange, but I really didn't think much of it at the time!"

Paul, Craig, and Sonya looked surprised; they exchanged glances at one another.

"Nikki! Do you remember what the guys looked like?"

Sonya asked me.

I thought back to the evening of the wedding, and I saw one with a black cap and the other one had... The other one had a tattoo of the red lady.

"One of the guys was the young employee from the gun store, and the one with the ball cap was Ivan!"

They were surprised again, the look on their faces like they had been slapped.

"We need to go speak to that other employee."

Paul remarked.

"Nikki, I have to go. I can have an officer take you back to your car."

"Ok, sure!"

Just then, another call came in on the police radio.

"Be advised that all units are available to a car crash on Palm Ave, a black sedan with license plate 2AY45LP, a victim shot."

"Are you thinking what I'm thinking?"

Sonya asked Paul.

"It's him!" Craig shouted.

"Yeah, let's go! Nikki, I need you to identify him!"

"All right!" I replied, running along for the ride.

Sonya and Craig left in her black SUV, with her red and blue lights flashing!

Paul and I left in his cruiser, and we followed suit with lights and sirens two blocks over on Palm Ave.

When we arrived, we saw the black sedan had crashed into a light pole; two pedestrians had flagged us down.

"We called it in. We were just walking home from the movie theatre, and we saw this guy drive like he was swerving, and then he hit the light pole."

The witnesses, a couple in their early 50s, told us. They were a little shaken up.

"You did fine. Please have a seat on the bench, and we can interview you. Thank you for your help."

Sonya instructed the witnesses.

We had another Cavalry of backup cops, paramedics, and more crime scene investigators coming to help. We reached the vehicle, and Paul did warn me I might puke. He opened the front door with gloved hands. The paramedics went first to check for a pulse, and they shook their heads no!

He was already dead.

I looked over and saw the employee from the gun store. Roxi and I saw yesterday. He was dressed all in black, his shades broken, with only one side of the glasses hanging from the side of his face. The airbag had deployed, and he looked as if he were just sleeping.

His hand was hanging down by his seat belt, and I asked Paul to pull up his sleeve. There was the tattoo of the lady in red, and I also noticed the gunshot to the chest point-blank.

"Is he the same man you saw at the hotel that day?" Paul asked me.

I nodded to him and barely spoke, "That's him!"

He led me away from the car and sat me down on a bench next to the other witnesses. I took some small breaths and gained my composure. My breath was visible in the air from the low and chilly temps.

Craig and Sonya began interviewing the couple; they were clearly shaken up. After fifteen minutes, they had another officer take them home.

I got in the cruiser, and Paul drove me home. He said he would call me tomorrow and check in on me. He didn't stay long; I knew he had to get back to the crime scene.

I put on my warm jammies, brushed my teeth, and went to bed!

***

I woke up early the next morning, after my daily routine, I went to the kitchen and made coffee and breakfast.

So now the case takes a turn, I thought over every piece of the case.

1. Three people are dead! Is there a connection to Rancho Arms and Tactical? They all worked for Vic.

2. Who shot the guy who killed Jack?

3. Did any one of those guys steal the guns and place them at the gallery?

4. These victims have another connection. What is it?

I thought that over for a moment. What else do these guys have as a common denominator? Something was missing.

Paul sent me a text.

"Good morning, I've had about four hours of sleep. How are you holding up?"

"Not too bad, considering! I do have a question for you, Paul. What was the name of the guy in the black sedan?"

"His name is Sergey Noble. He's a student at Cal State Rancho Niguel, and of course, you know he worked at Rancho Arms and Tactical."

"We do know that all three took loans from Vic, the owner. I interviewed some people who knew the victims. They say Vic is a loan shark, like the mob."

"Do you think they stole from him, like retaliation? Maybe for paying back those loans with interest, or do you think they were still doing jobs for him, favors?"

"I think there is still another missing link that we haven't covered yet," Paul replied.

"That makes sense; we still don't know how the guns wound up at the art gallery."

"That's the part that bothers me; we have no connection with the gallery and with Vic. Ivan, Jack, and Sergey."

"Yeah, I know, Paul. It's not like any of them worked for Martin and Oliver; all of their part-time employees are in the art world, or they are students..." Wait a minute, students!

"Paul, were Ivan and Jack students? Did they go to CSURN(Cal State University Rancho Niguel)?"

He paused for a moment as if going through his trusty little notebook.

"Yes, they did! Nikki, you found the link!"

"Paul! Martin and Oliver's employee, Lindo, attends CSURN! He has keys to the gallery, he knows the building, and he is the..." I trailed off, then said:

"The one who usually accepts all of the shipments."

"I need to talk to him!"

"I'm coming with you!"

Before he could garner a protest, I hung up, grabbed my keys, and headed to the art gallery.

118

It was chilly outside, so I took my black ultralight 850 hooded jacket. Thanks again, LL Bean.

Lightweight and very warm.

It was cloudy outside, with temperatures at 40 degrees right now. On the way, I called Martin and Oliver. They had told me they were cleaning today, and they had all hands on deck, so I knew Lindo would be there.

The mall was already crowded with customers shopping during the last couple of days before Christmas. It was hard to find a parking spot, and I was worried I wouldn't get one.

Oh, that's right, the Christmas parade was going to be at noon today, no wonder there was so much traffic. I had forgotten about that!

I would have walked over, but it was so chilly out that I thought my legs would freeze before I got to the art gallery.

The streets were blocked off, three to be exact! Some concrete barriers were put in to protect parade spectators, the parade floats, and entertainers. Police presence was abundant, and fire trucks and medics were in the parade, so they were there as well.

Parents and kids were now setting up their folding chairs in place along the sidewalk, and a coffee cart was traveling up and down the parade route selling hot chocolate, coffee, tea, and warm cider.

The city had put up garlands, with large red and gold ornaments on them, around the city light poles that lined the streets in the outdoor mall. The mall gazebo, decorated with a red velvet drape over it, had Santa and his large wooden chair set up for photos, and some food trucks parked in the common area, open for selling their wonderful dishes.

Mexican food, Burgers, sushi, Pho soups, Curries, BBQ, Chowder, and many more food establishments were here, as well as a dessert truck selling pumpkin pie, peppermint cheesecakes, fudge, cookies, and peppermint bark. Yummy, I'm going to have to stay for this.

I reached the art gallery and knocked on the glass door. I saw Martin, and he came to the door to open it.

"Hi Nikki, what are you doing here? Did you come to help out?" He smiled.

"Martin, I need to talk to you and Oliver, it's important!" He saw the urgency on my face; he let me in, and just as I did, Paul showed up.

"Martin gave me a strange look.

"What's going on, Nikki?"

"I'll explain all of it, but first, is Lindo here?"

"We need to talk to him!" Paul explained.

"He's in the basement."

Oliver and Lindo were coming up from downstairs, a large bucket and a mop in his hands. Oliver smiled, but then frowned when he saw Paul. "Nikki, what's going on?"

I walked right up to Lindo and pulled him aside against the wall, cornering him.

"Lindo, do you have something you would like to tell us?" I asked while giving him the truth-telling look that I knew he was hiding something from us.

His expression of fear came over him, and now he took a deep breath and doubled over, his face full of sorrow.

"I can't do zes anymore; I am so sorry, Mar-tin and o-li-ver!" He covered his face and began to sob. Martin and Oliver's faces were lit with shock and confusion; they looked to me and then to Paul for an answer.

"Lindo, tell me what you know. How deep in this are you?" Paul questioned.

Lindo's story unfolded with tears and regret; I had to listen very closely to him now, his thick accent making it difficult to understand some of his sentences. Paul had to have him take deep breaths and calm down. I guess he was having a hard time getting the story out.

We all sat down in the lobby on the sofa, and he spilled the beans! Lindo told us that when he came here to this country to go to school, he didn't have a lot of money, and he took some odd jobs here and there until he found the art gallery.

He said that at one time, he took a loan from Vic because his classmate Ivan (yes, the one who was killed) told him about getting a loan for school and living expenses.

Lindo took the loan, but after 10 weeks, he paid it all back with interest. He thought he was finally on his way to his American dream when, out of the blue in October, Vic called him and asked him to do him a favor.

Vic wanted Lindo to accept a few shipments of products to the art gallery; he said it was for some gifts for friends of his out in Long Beach, but that he couldn't have them go to the Rancho Arms and Tactical because he was under surveillance.

He told Lindo that if he refused to do this favor, it would be considered disrespectful, and he would pay. His American dream would be taken away.

Lindo agreed. He said he thought it was just two boxes; he had no idea what was in them because Vic never told him. He figured he would do the favor, and then Vic would leave him alone.

Then, when Vic asked him to store the guns, Lindo said no, he was done with this! Vic punched him in the gut and told him next time, it would be a knife to the gut, not a fist.

So Lindo stored the guns downstairs, but had no idea that someone would call the police to tell them the guns were in the basement. Lindo said he wanted to go to the police; he wanted to tell Paul that day that Martin and Oliver were arrested, but that he was afraid of Vic. He also said that morning, Vic reminded him to keep his mouth shut by putting a dead bird on his front door.

Lindo was sorry, and he asked Martin and Oliver to forgive him. He told Paul he was genuinely afraid of Vic and feared that he would end up like Ivan.

"Lindo, we can protect you. We can tell the DA all of this, and you can get immunity, you won't go to jail." Paul reassured him.

"You should have come to us.

We would have gone to Paul right away, and Vic wouldn't have been able to force you to do this!"

Oliver said to Lindo.

"Lindo, if you can get Vic to incriminate himself as the one behind the whole operation, we have him."

Lindo agreed, Paul said he could have him wear a wire to get Vic to talk about this and threaten him, so it would all be under surveillance.

"Lindo, does Vic have a tattoo of a lady in a red dress?"

"Yes, on his arm." He said between sobs.

"What does that mean?" I asked Paul.

Martin and Oliver turned their attention to Paul for his response as well.

"It means he's part of the Russian Mafia; the lady in red represents Mother Russia! The organization is called The Family Krasny. In Russian, it means red or beautiful. We have an officer at the department who is a Russian immigrant; he said organizations like this are in the belief of the old Russian KGB.

Most of these mafias are crime syndicates that, for them, the Cold War is still going on."

Wow! I was surprised! All of this is in Rancho Niguel!

Martin and Oliver were, too; they had been pretty silent, just listening to everything Lindo told us.

"Paul, now don't get upset. Roxi and I have a class at Rancho Arms and Tactical!"

"What were you thinking, Nikki? This guy is a killer!" Paul said, frustrated.

"We just wanted to see his store, see if anything seemed off. That's all! But if we cancel, it might tip him off, don't you think? Plus, everyone knows that I have helped with solving crimes."

Paul made a face, indicating he wasn't happy with my meddling. He thought for a moment and pinched the bridge of his nose, then he said.

"Keep your class; I will have Lindo call him afterward and set up a meeting. This way, he's not tipped off that something is up, and you and Roxi won't be around him."

"Okay, our class is at 2 pm there at the store."

"Lindo, you'll come with me so my team can get you ready for the meeting. At 3 pm, call him and tell him you want to talk to him, you need money, or you're going to the police.

We will have a place where you will meet him and plenty of officers all around."

Lindo looked apprehensive about doing this, but he realized it was death or maybe prison if they didn't catch Vic in the act.

"Ok, I will do zit!" He said, feeling defeated.

Martin and Oliver felt bad for Lindo, so they called their lawyer and told her everything they had just talked about.

They said she would be representing Lindo, the lawyer wanted to meet with Paul before anything went down, and wanted Lindo's testimony to have immunity on paper.

Paul agreed but said he needed the DA's approval, which should be no problem.

He said the charges against Martin and Oliver would be dropped, and they would be fully free of any wrongdoing. We had a plan in motion!

Chapter 13

Ready, Aim, Fire

Paul and Lindo left to go to the station to get him wired and to coach him on his meeting with Vic. Martin and Oliver were going with him for support. I had to go pick up Roxi and then get to our class. I left the gallery, but getting out was going to be harder than I thought.

Families were now lined up on the sidewalk watching the parade; I had to squeeze past people and try to get back to my car. On the way out, I managed to see part of the parade walking down Main Street.

Rancho Niguel High School's band was playing "Jingle Bells." Majorettes, flag tossers, and drill team members were smiling brightly, walking down the street to the beat of the song. All dressed in festive uniforms, the school colors of royal blue, white, and gold, they wore red Santa hats on their heads and white boots with dangling snowballs made of yarn.

Behind them was a float from Bon Voyage Travel Agency, an old 1957 Chevy Nomad Wagon in Tropical Turquoise was decorated with a green wreath on the front of it.

Next was the West Rancho Niguel High School Eagles band, majorettes, drill dance team, and flags, sporting the red, white, and silver. The athletes walked behind the drill team, and I spotted two athletes I recognized, the boy and girl who went into Coco Jo's the other day. They cheered and tossed candy canes to the kids on the sidewalk. I was almost close to my car, and I had to squeeze again through some high schoolers, wearing red and white, no doubt West RN students.

The boy from Coco Jo's turned his attention to one of the boys on the sidewalk, one of his fellow schoolmates, and the two had cold, hard stares at one another. That was strange, I thought, maybe just teen problems.

I reached my car and got in. I navigated slowly and finally made it out of the mall and back home.

I called Roxi and told her I would be by her place in five minutes. I asked her for the fourth time, "Are you sure you want to do this?"

"Roxi is!"

"You were so nervous the other day, what's the change?"

"I realized I have to face fear straight on, so I won't be afraid of it. I'm a strong woman, and I want to learn to defend myself!"

"I'm so proud of you, Roxi!"

I wasn't sure what to prepare for, but I made sure my phone was fully charged and that I wore my boots with a strong, hard toe. I got to Roxi's, and we were off to our class. She was confident and ready to conquer!

I hadn't told Roxi about anything that happened at the gallery; I just figured the less she knew, the better we were. I would tell her after Vic was arrested. The plan was simple: Roxi and I would go to the class along with six other ladies, and the class ended at 3 pm. Roxi and I leave, and the moment we drive away, I send Paul a text saying we're home safe, and then Lindo calls Vic and asks for a meeting at the park at 3:30 pm!

We walked into Ranch Arms and Tactical, and six other females were gathered around, ready for their introduction to firearms! We all introduced ourselves and said hello. Vic was there along with two other employees; they wore short-sleeved black shirts, but neither one had a Russian mafia tattoo. Vic led us upstairs, and the other two employees stayed to help customers in the store. Once in the range, we were given eye protection glasses and ear protective muffs, and we were paired off in groups of two. Roxi and I were assigned to station 3.

We all sat in a classroom first to go over safety rules.

Vic stood at the front of the room, writing his rules on the white easel. In bright green marker, he scribbled.

"Ladies, this is very important; you must follow these rules and guidelines. First, I will go over the rules for firearms. Next, I will go over range rules."

1. **Treat all firearms as if they are loaded.**

2. **Never put your finger on the trigger until you are going to shoot.**

3. **Never point a gun at anyone unless you are shooting them.**

4. **Be sure of your target and what's beyond it.**

He listed about five more rules and then went on to the range rules.

1. **Make sure you have your eye and ear protection on.**

2. **Make sure you keep your gun on the table until it is your turn to shoot.**

3. **Only one shooter at a time in the lane.**

4. **The other person must stay behind the white line behind the shooter at all times when the shooter is shooting.**

5. **Cold range means guns down, no shooting.**

6. Hot range means shooting has commenced.

7. If your gun gets jammed, put the gun down immediately and call me or the range master.

After a few more rules, we got up and went over to the lanes; each handgun was sitting on the small counter in the lanes. Each firearm had the magazine removed and placed beside it. The gun was racked back and open to show that there was no ammunition in the chamber.

We each went to our stations, and Vic showed us targets and where and how to shoot at them. We went over where our sights were on the gun in order to aim correctly. We learned about target groupings and how that plays an important role in how we wound our assailant!

We learned how to load a magazine with the ammunition brought over by the Range Master. We were taught how to hold the firearm, how to stand, and when to breathe! We each had a chance to load seven rounds in the magazine.

Once we were done with that, we placed the magazine in the firearm, and then Vic and the Range Master showed us how to rack the gun. We put our safety glasses on and laid the gun down on the counter in front of us.

Roxi was up first. She got into her stance and made sure her ear protection was secured and her glasses were on. She waited until Vic told us to pick up our weapons.

 "Range Hot. Pick up your guns, aim forward, release the safety, and fire."

I stood behind the line while I watched Roxi fire her weapon. She seemed very confident, her posture was perfect, and she followed all of the rules.

When the rounds of 7 were shot, all of the women put down their firearms and stepped back from the lane.

"Range Cold, guns down," Vic shouted.

The targets automatically moved forward to us, and we changed them out. Roxi's groupings were all in the right chest area. We switched places, and then it was my turn. I placed a new target on and sent it back. I followed the same directions for loading as Roxi did.

"Ladies, don't worry about picking up the casings, we will take care of that." The Range Master said.

"Range Hot pick up your guns, aim forward, release the safety, and fire."

Vic said once again.

I focused on the aim, the thump, thump of the sound of the bullets hitting my target. When I was out, I put down my gun and waited for the others to finish.

"Range Cold, guns down."

When my target came forward, I took it down and marveled over my performance: five in the center, two a few inches left.

Vic and the Range Master came over to our station.

"She has a near-perfect!" The Range Master commented

"Yes, it is impressive, Ms. Rodriguez!"

"Beginner's luck!" I grinned foolishly.

When we shot our last round again, we all put down our weapons and returned to the classroom.

The range Master passed out certificates of completion for our participation in the class. Vic wasn't around; I guess he was needed downstairs.

We all congratulated each other and said goodbye! Roxi and I were headed downstairs when the Range Master asked us to stay. He said Vic wanted to congratulate us away from everyone else and wanted to offer us another class at no charge. Roxi and I looked at each other, not quite knowing what to do.

Vic came back upstairs, and the Range Master left.

I knew the plan was for Roxi and me to leave as soon as possible.

"Vic, thank you for a wonderful class," Roxi stated.

"Yes, Vic, it was a pleasure. Roxi and I do have another appointment to get to, so we should be leaving."

He was blocking the doorway now and just stood there silently.

Roxi looked at me with a *what is going on look*.

"About that class for free, we have such a busy schedule right now because of the holidays, but maybe in the new year, we can see if it fits our calendar."

I moved forward towards the open doorway, but he didn't move! Again, I thought we were trapped in the classroom; we had no escape.

"Ms. Rodriguez, I can't let you and Ms. Carmichael leave, you know too much!"

"What are you talking about?" Roxi asked.

"She doesn't know anything, just let her go!"

"I can't do that; you made her a liability, too!"

I had my jacket on, and one hand was in my pocket with my phone.

Vic grabbed us and led us out to the range floor, forcing us to the ground. He turned and walked over to the outer door leading to the staircase; his back was turned, so I took out my phone and sent a HELP text to Paul.

I pressed record on my phone and stashed it on the floor behind a small trash can by one of the lanes. Vic had looked out on the main floor. Back and forth, craning his neck to make sure the coast was clear down below.

He looked back at us, then went to a small closet, opened it, and removed some rope and tape. I wasn't sure if he was taking us someplace or if he was just going to leave us tied up here while he made his getaway.

When he came back, he said, "Everyone is gone, so no one can hear you scream!"

"What are you going to do with us?" Roxi asked, her expression scared and worried.

"You will be my insurance, so I can leave with no problems. The police will come soon, and I need hostages. I will make my demands, and then I will leave the country."

The Range master came back up holding a gun and a big gulp.

"What is this?" Vic asked, pointing to the XXL Big Gulp filled with what looked to be Cherry Coke.

He handed a handgun to Vic now!

"I am thirsty, you know I love Cherry Coke."

He told Vic.

"Don't get sloppy,"

Vic told him while rolling his eyes at his behavior.

"Did you take their phones?"

Mr. XXL Big Gulp asked, sipping away!

"Not yet, but I've been watching them the whole time."

The Range Master came up to us, "Let's have them!"

Roxi opened her small purse and handed it over

He pointed the gun at me, but I told him

"I left mine in the car!" I handed him my keys.

"Go out and get it !" Vic told the Range Master.

"Ok!" He said and left downstairs.

"Vic, I know you conned Lindo into hiding those guns for you and for receiving your shipments."

"He has been useful, but now I must eliminate him too!"

"Why did you kill Ivan, Jack, and Sergey?"

Roxi's eyes grew large with surprise. She had little information right now, and everything would be a revelation for her!

"They had become more liabilities for my operation, and now so have you." He pointed the gun at us.

"But why? Who are you running guns for?"

"For this!"

He rolled up his sleeve and showed me his tattoo, another lady in red.

"The family, Krasny!

I have been sending guns and supplies to my comrades through the port to Finland and then by boat to a small island called Red Isle, where the KGB has intercepted them; we now have a large supply to take back what is ours!

Yes, we will bring back the Cold War; it was never really over! You Americans are so entitled to your freedom and your patriotic liberty! Russia will be stronger than ever before; it is a shame you will not see it!"

He was full of pride and confidence, but it kept him talking, and hopefully, my phone was recording all of his confessions.

"Ivan lost his loyalty to his country; instead, he wanted to be like an American, he wanted to be free! No more war! He said I want to finish school and be an engineer. And that Sergey wanted to leave too! He had a scholarship for next semester and a new American girlfriend, but I said after you take out Jack, you can go!"

"Why did you have Jack killed?" I asked, stalling.

"I killed Jack; he was going to the cops, and that Sergey, he backed out at the last minute, so I shot him. After that, I took his car and killed Jack! I put Sergey's body in the car, put his foot on the gas pedal, and then, with his keyless remote, I started the car. It ran into a pole.

"The police found his key in the car with him!" I stated.

"They found one key; he had two, and I took the other one back to his apartment."

"Who did the robberies for you? Was that Sergey?"

"That was some stupid kids I sell pot to; I saw them breaking into the stores. So I break into mine, so it looks like they did it!"

"Why would you want people to think guns were stolen from you? And why did you leave those guns at the art gallery?"

"To make it look like Ivan was stealing from the store, as I said before, I sent those guns to my comrades. I had to make it look like they were missing from the inventory, stolen by someone. Otherwise, the police would know what I was doing."

"But they only found three!" I asked him.

"I had to make it look like Ivan was working with someone else. This would send the police on a big chase, and by the time they understood what happened, the guns and I would be in Russia!"

"You're not going to get away with it!"

Roxi said, anger filling her soft voice.

Vic smirked, a sly, slick look on his face, no doubt congratulating himself on his brilliant plan.

We heard someone coming up the stairs; the Range Master would be back and know that I had lied. Oh, man! I wondered where Paul was. Did he get my message? What if his phone was off or on silent mode? He had been so busy getting Lindo prepared for his big meeting.

"Nikki Rodriguez, you ask too many questions!"

He pointed the gun at me. "I think I will shoot you first."

Roxi and I sat silently next to each other; she grabbed my hand!

"Put the gun down!" Paul came up the stairs with two other officers and four ATF agents. They all had their guns drawn; they surrounded Vic, took his gun, and cuffed him.

"Are you guys ok?" Paul holstered his gun and then picked me up off the ground in a big hug! Roxi hugged both of us.

"I'm glad to see you," I told him.

"I got everything on record, too!" I bent down to retrieve my phone and showed him the 10-minute recording.

We walked downstairs; there were police, ATF, and some guys in black suits all standing around at some kind of base camp that was set up. The street was blocked off with barricades, and some tables and chairs had been brought in under a white tent. Roxi and I sat down at a table; Paul gave us a bottle of water to drink.

We saw the Range Master and Vic being led away in a Government white van.

"Where are they taking those two?"

I asked Paul.

"ATF has them in custody; it's their show now!"

"So how did Vic know that we were on to him?"

I asked Paul.

"Somehow, the media got a tip that we were going to go after Vic today. One of our undercover officers was staking out the place. He saw a news van parked in the back alley and saw Vic spot them. Most likely, he put two and two together. First, we had you both going in the store, and then when all of the ladies from the class were led out, we knew you two were still in the building, and then I got a text that read HELP from you. It was obvious something was wrong!"

"So, who tipped off the media?" I asked.

"We don't know! The only thing I can say is that four people in the department knew, and I trust them all: Craig, Sonya, Chief, and me! Someone at the department may have overheard our conversation, or maybe they realized what was happening when ATF officers came by the station."

Roxi and I just listened and tried to put everything into perspective.

"Girl, I'm telling you, I thought we were goners, I was so scared!"

"Me too, Roxi. I was worried."

"It was a smart idea to tell Vic you left your phone in the car. The moment the Range Master came out, we knew we had a way in."

It was getting cold out here, and I was ready to go inside and warm up.

A man in a black suit walked up to us.

"Ms. Rodriguez, here is your phone. We took what we needed and erased it from your phone. Thank you for your duty to your country; we appreciate it."

With that, he left in a black sedan with two other men in black.

Chapter 14

Oh Christmas Tree

The national news picked up the story about the bust, but my name and Roxi's were kept out of it. Paul said it was safer that way; no one needed a reason to come after us. He was still upset that the information was leaked and could have led to Roxi and me being killed. He said he would find out who was at fault. They only reported the police investigation into the murders and the gun theft. The other stuff was left out due to national security.

We dropped Roxi off at home, and then Paul and I went to get some takeout. After a plate of ham, mashed potatoes, gravy, green beans, and a slice of apple pie from Stella's Coffee Shop! I was ready for bed.

I woke up rejuvenated the next day! The local news had the arrest of Vic Parker, AKA Viktor Slovak, his real name.

Lindo struck a deal to testify against Vic and was offered full immunity. Because of the national security that was at stake, Lindo was to go into witness protection.

They couldn't be sure Vic was the only Russian asset around here, so they insisted. Wow, another person in witness protection. What is it with Rancho Niguel?

I had just three days until Christmas, and I didn't even have a Christmas tree! I decided I had to get one today! I was in the Christmas spirit, Martin and Oliver were cleared of all charges, Paul and the officers of Rancho Niguel caught the bad guys, and now it was time to celebrate.

Although there still was the mystery of who committed the robberies at Coco Jo's and Lady Grays' Tea Shoppe! Vic had mentioned some kids he sold pot to. Then, there was the mystery of who tipped off the press. Paul said he was looking into that. I knew he was very angry about it, and it also begged the question: was it an inside job?

I called Paul to see if maybe he could give me a lift to get my tree. He has a Toyota Tundra truck in Army Green he bought last year. It's a cool truck with a lot of towing power and cool extras.

I left a message for him to call me, but it seems like he is probably still busy. A few seconds later, I got a text that read.

Sorry, I can't talk right now.

I'm working on something.

At work. I'll call you tonight.

Babe.

So after that bummer, I called a friend...

Matt picked me up fifteen minutes after I called him. He was off today and happy to help.

"Thank you for the help today."

"It's no problem; I wasn't doing very much at home, just organizing my kitchen pantry." He laughed.

We pulled into Santiagos Tree Farm, an actual cut-your-own tree-down kind of place, complete with an ax and twine. This place is nestled at the entrance of the mountain area above Rancho Niguel on your way up to Big Bear.

"I'll let you carry the ax, Matt, you have more experience with it than I do."

It was about ten degrees colder up here, and some of the trees had a light dusting of frost. We went down several aisles of trees, small, tall, wide, slender, sparse, and full.

"What kind of tree did you get, Matt?"

144

"I thought I would take advantage of my high ceilings, so I went with a 12-foot tree, a Noble fir."

"Wow! That's cool, have you decorated it yet?"

"Yeah."

"Do you think you can help me decorate my tree? I'll make you dinner as a thank you for it."

"How can I say no to a home-cooked meal?" He smiled.

We turned the corner, and there it was, my tree, a six-foot-tall Douglas fir.

"So, were you involved in yesterday's arrest of Vic, the Russian dude?" He asked.

"Yes!" I reluctantly admitted.

"How did you know Matt? Our names were kept out of the story."

"I had a feeling."

I told Matt everything that happened yesterday while he chopped my tree down for me.

"Nikki, you are a unique person, but darlin', please be careful."

"I think this was my last adventure with Nikki, the amateur sleuth. I promise I'm staying away from trouble!"

I paid for the tree, had a stand put on it, and Matt put it in the back of his truck with some tie-downs.

Santiago's Farm had a small coffee stand, and I bought Matt and me some peppermint bark hot chocolates with mini marshmallows.

"Thank you, I needed this." He smiled, taking a sip.

"You know me, I never turn down chocolate."

I said, taking a sip.

We got back to my place, and Matt brought the tree inside. He placed it in the living room for me in the corner and added water to the tree stand.

I had my boxes of decorations stacked up in the dining room. I put some Christmas music on my TV from my Pandora app and turned on the fireplace.

I brought the boxes over and took out the lights. Matt strung them up for me. I brought out my ornaments, some from when I was a kid and some new ones that I had recently purchased.

"I was looking for this!" Matt said, surprised.

He picked up a small round ornament that looked like a 3-inch slice of wood, with a red heart in the middle of it and our initials N and M on each side of the heart. With the date printed underneath the heart and green holly bordering the ornament.

He stopped and held it in his hand, thinking back on a memory.

"I thought I lost this."

"Remember, that year we had Christmas at the station, and you didn't have a Christmas tree that year because you had three people out sick, and you basically lived at the station that month. I had that made as our first ornament."

"This was from the Girl Scouts fundraiser; they sold ornaments that year. The local troop mom was one of those crafty women who had a wood-burning engraver tool, and she personalized all of them. That was also the year we had a lot of brush fires along the freeway from that serial arsonist. I was so glad when we caught him." Matt said.

"That was quite a year."

"Remember we had that heat wave in December, too!" I replied.

I let Matt finish decorating the tree; he placed our ornament in the middle of the tree so it was the first one you could see if you looked at the tree.

I went into the kitchen to start dinner, and I opened the fridge and spotted some pork chops. I know what I'm cooking.

Pork chops in a creamy mushroom garlic sauce, cranberry pecan salad, and parsnip puree.

I went to work; I grilled my chops in butter. I boiled my parsnips. When the chops were done, I put them aside. I began my sauce, sautéed some onion, garlic, thyme, and mushrooms, and added salt and pepper. When they were golden, I added white wine to deglaze, and then 1/2 cup of beef broth, simmered it all for a few minutes, and next, I added heavy cream.

Boom done. Just like that!

I placed the chops back in the pan to simmer on very low for a few minutes.

I put the soft parsnips in the blender and then added salt and pepper. I put them in a Le Creuset ceramic dish and then added butter on top with chopped Italian parsley. I took out some mixed salad greens and dried cranberries, diced pecans, and some crumbled feta. I made an apple vinaigrette dressing to go with it. I placed everything on the dining table, grabbed some wine glasses, and called Matt to the table.

"Time to eat!"

The music on Pandora played "Sleigh Ride" by Ella Fitzgerald.

"Oh my God, that looks fantastic!"

Matt said, washing up in the kitchen sink.

He rolled up his flannel shirt sleeves and sat down to eat.

"I haven't had time to cook lately, and I forgot how much I enjoy it," I replied.

I sat down and placed my red cloth napkin across my lap, digging in and then serving the red wine, one from Educated Guess. One of my favorite Cabernet Sauvignon wines from Napa, California.

As we ate, our conversation shifted to relationships. Matt put his fork down and wiped his mouth; he had something on his mind.

"I was wondering, well, we never finished our conversation from our phone call."

He trailed off.

I knew what he was asking me. I put my fork down now, too. I swallowed what I had in my mouth and silently took a breath. I had to fess up to it. He was so considerate all of the time, tactful and compassionate. How much truth was I going to tell him, right down to what had bothered me months ago but now didn't seem so important to reason?

I looked at him, his kind face giving me full attention, his eyes calm.

"Right before we discussed moving in together, I... I've always seen the way women were trying to grab your attention or flirt with you, and I know you never encouraged any of it; you were honest with me. My trust issues with relationships made me feel that, at some point, I just wouldn't be enough.

It would have been difficult losing you to someone else; I didn't want to be hurt! When you were dating Summer Simmons, I was crazy with jealousy, even though I told everyone I was ok with you moving on, but inside, my heart was breaking! Matt, I see you, and I light up inside. You make me smile.

The thing is that now I have Paul, and I love him too, just in a different way! Our relationship is not as intense the way it is with you! Matt, I have loved you from the first day we met!"

Then I pulled him in for a long kiss.

But that's not what happened, and that's not what I told him! Instead, I broke from my daydream or fantasy, and I chickened out and said this instead:

"Our relationship was moving too fast for me, and I felt like I couldn't catch my breath. I needed some time to myself to assess everything I was doing. I didn't want you to just wait around for me. I didn't think that was fair to you, so I just thought we were better off apart."

"So this relationship with Anderson, how serious is it?"

"We are taking everything very slow right now; we are just having fun, enjoying the company of each other, and trying new things. I mean, my gosh, I surf right now, can you believe that?"

I laughed.

"So it's nothing serious?" He asked.

"Like I said, we are good friends, just dating and getting to know each other, I'm not looking at wedding rings or searching for my wedding dress, ok."

"Yeah, that's what I thought, nothing serious."

He seemed convinced and genuinely understanding of what I told him. We finished our meal, and Matt complimented it several times.

"It's too bad you never owned a restaurant, your cooking is amazing!"

"Yeah, well, maybe someday." I smiled, keeping my secret to myself about owning Kendle's.

He helped me clear the dishes and put them in the dishwasher. I love a man who is helpful in the kitchen. What a turn on Ha-ha.

I didn't have any dessert here in the house, but I asked Matt if he wanted some tea or coffee.

"I'm sorry, I don't have any dessert here. Would you like some coffee or tea?"

"No, that's fine, I'm so full from dinner, it's probably better that I don't have any."

"So, do you have any plans for Christmas?" I asked him.

"Christmas Eve, I'll be at the station, and then most likely Christmas Day too."

"Maybe I'll come by and bring you some food."

"That would be nice." He liked that idea.

I decided to change the subject and shift to something that would keep us from looking dreamily into each other's eyes.

"So I heard that the police still don't know who pulled off those robberies."

"I'm sure Paul will find out who did them; he is good at his job." Matt complimented him.

Vic did say that he spotted some kids in the act, and that is what gave him the idea to move the guns. I didn't mention this to Matt, but it kept circling my mind: the kids, the teens from Coco Jo's that day I was there talking to Joanne.

"Matt, do you know anything about a youth center that is supposed to be in the works for the community?"

"As a matter of fact, I was approached by Stacie Mc. Daniel's the mayor's assistant, and she asked me if I would like to be a part of it. I told her yes, I think being a mentor to kids is a wonderful way for me to give back to my community and help some kids find their way. I told her I'm on board with it."

"Are they building a new place for this?"

"She said the only thing holding them back is the money to build an addition to the community center, or maybe a new location, a new building."

"Hmm, is that so!"

Just then, my phone chimed out.

"Rockin' Around The Christmas Tree."

"Hello!"

"Nikki, it's Paul. I was wondering if you needed some company right now." Oh, man! I looked over at Matt, putting the tree skirt around the bottom of the tree, and then he looked at our ornament again.

"I uh... I'm a little tired right now. I was going to turn in early."

"Oh, ok."

I felt bad. Paul and I hadn't had any time to see each other, and by the sound of his voice, maybe he needed a friend.

"How about in an hour, we can maybe go grab some pie and coffee."

"Ok, I'll pick you up in an hour." I was away from Matt's ear, walking down my hallway to my room.

"That sounds great, see ya."

Now, I had to get Matt to leave.

I walked back to the living room; Matt was very intelligent, and I think he already knew what I was going to ask.

"Nikki, I'd better get going. I'm pretty beat, and the next few days are usually crazy, so I should get some sleep."

"Thank you for going with me today. The tree looks beautiful."

"Thank you for dinner, it was wonderful."

He walked to the door, pulled his coat from the closet, and put it on.

"I hope the Winter Ball is a huge success. I would have bought a ticket, but I have to work tomorrow night, too."

"Oh, that's fine, I know how much you support me and the community."

Here come the butterflies again in my stomach, I could feel my heart beating faster, and my eyes got glossy. What is this called again?

"I had a wonderful time today, thank you."

Matt leaned over and kissed me.

A long kiss that made me feel light-headed and happy all at the same time. His heart is beating just as fast as mine. I felt loved and calm like everything in the world was going to be fine...

Chapter 15

Baby, It's Cold Outside.

Paul was right on time; he knocked on the door 60 minutes after his phone call.

"Hi, come on in!"

"It's freezing outside!" He rubbed his hands together and walked in. He was right, the temperature had dropped again, and this evening was bringing in the chill!

We decided to go to Kendl's for dessert. I called ahead and had Chef Stark prepare us his famous Apple spice cake with cream cheese frosting. He had made several of them that were going to be donated to St. Mark's Catholic Church for their holiday dinner. We had put aside three loaves of cake for the staff to munch on before the Winter Ball.

Ken, the part-time bartender, was working this evening. I had offered him an assistant management position so Tito and Daisy could keep business hours.

They usually traded off days, nights, and weekends; I left their schedule up to them, it didn't matter what shifts they worked as long as we had coverage.

I gave them a lot of flexibility with scheduling staff, too. I wanted happy people working here, and if they needed time off, it was always granted. This isn't a prison; we can all help out and give each other time away.

We sat by the fireplace at a window seat booth. We drank coffee to warm up. The house music was playing, Kenny G Christmas jazz.

"So, Paul, have you found out who tipped off the press about the arrest?"

"I'm still looking into it; I know whoever it is will be fired!"

Our cake arrived, and we decided not to talk shop.

"I'm excited about the Winter Ball tomorrow we have everything ready, the chef has prepared a wonderful dinner: roasts, mashed potatoes, sautéed vegetables, seafood dishes, clams, shrimp scampi, hours D' over's of stuffed mushrooms, canapés, caviar with crackers, smoked salmon, dips, you name it the spread is going to be fabulous!"

"I can't wait, it sounds wonderful." He smiled.

I was biting my nails trying to bring this up; I wanted to just get to the point.

"Paul, a few days ago, I saw you at Blue 7 with Stacie. You two are spending a lot of time together. What's going on?"

Subtlety was not my specialty!

"Nikki, I swear I'm being straight with you. Stacie and I are just collaborating on the business with the youth center. I'm not going to lie, I'm flattered by your jealousy," He teased.

"Me! Jealous! Never." I teased back.

" I've been giving her a lot of ideas and making some suggestions that she's happy with. The youth center is going to be big; it will provide so many positive outlets for our community."

He finished saying.

"Vic had told me that he saw some kids breaking into the two businesses that night they were robbed."

I offered up in the conversation.

"We don't have any proof that what he said was true; there weren't any indications of who the thieves were, they were wearing masks and dark clothing."

"You know, Paul, something has been bugging me since I saw it. I was shopping the day of the robberies at Coco Jo's, and I saw these two teenagers walk in, and for some reason, they just seemed off."

I explained, trying to put a fine point on what I was conveying!

"Tell me more."

Paul was listening intently.

"These two teens were looking at the most expensive items in the store, the pots and the knives, the ones that are worth a lot. It seemed to me like they were casing the place."

"I can ask Joanne for her security cam footage and see if maybe they need to be brought in for questioning. I'll check it out, ok."

"Ok!"

I told him about the waves I caught a few days ago and my two wipeouts.

"I'm jealous; I wish I could have gone with you! You have become good at surfing, you know."

"Well, I did have a good teacher."

"How about Christmas Day? We go down and catch some waves."

"It's going to be freezing!" I replied.

"I'll get you a dry suit; you'll be fine."

"Maybe!"

We finished our dessert and coffee and went back to my place.

"I love your truck, man. Everyone has a truck; I might need to get myself one."

"Thanks, it's the only thing I purchased when I moved here. I'm looking at a condo or a house next; I'm tired of paying rent.

Plus, I need a garage for my stuff; my place is getting crammed, and now, with the truck, I don't want to park it outside anymore, the sun will damage the paint."

"My gosh, men and their garages!" I tsked.

"I think it would be fun to do yard work, maybe build a fence. I'm looking forward to homeownership." He looked hopeful.

"After seeing Matt's house last summer, it made me want to buy one, but I don't need all of that room right now, maybe in a few years," I told him.

"Well, don't wait too long, you can always sell it or rent it out."

"Yeah, maybe."

"I'll see you tomorrow then."

With that, we kissed goodnight, and he was off.

I was tossing and turning, trying to get comfortable, but I just couldn't. I was restless, and I didn't know why. I sat up in bed, my eyes tired but my mind running!

What could possibly be keeping me up? Often, I have attributed this to a sick sense, like when you just know that something is coming. Is it good? Maybe! Is it unexpected or a disappointment? Who knows, either way, I wasn't getting any sleep right now.

I turned on the TV, and White Christmas was on.

I just love the performances of the whole cast. Danny Kaye, Rosemary Clooney, Bing Crosby, and Vera-Ellen danced and sang. The song is called "sisters," and the part where Bing and Danny sing is oh-so-funny.

The beautiful costumes and the music, the sets. Wow, those were movies! I watched it all the way to the end, and then I fell right to sleep.

I woke up feeling rested, even though I had only five hours of sleep. I went to make some coffee, and I put some toast in my Breville oven. This oven is wonderful, it does everything from toast to air frying to baking, and it even broils.

I had a lot to do today with the Winter ball; it was going to be a long day. My first stop was going to be the dry cleaners to pick up my red dress for the ball. After breakfast, I was dressed and ready to go.

I started the bug and headed out. My phone chimed and went to my Bluetooth on the nav screen. "Hello, Chef Stark, what's up, dude?"

"Nikki, you need to get down here now. We have a busted pipe, and there is water everywhere!"

"What! Oh no! I'll be right there!"

When I arrived, Daisy and Tito were there with Chef Stark; he stood by with a long, sad look on his face.

"What happened, guys?"

"Nikki, when we arrived, we saw water all over the lobby and the dining room, and the kitchen was in a foot of water! We called you as soon as we turned the water off.

We called a plumber and had them come out immediately!

I went to the banquet room, and it, too, was flooded with a foot of water! I felt sick looking at the damage!

The plumber who arrived told us it looked like vandalism; the water pipe was busted!

"Yes, I've seen this before. You have a vandal. It was deliberately hit, maybe with a wrench or a hammer."

The plumber named Jody said, writing it up on his clipboard.

"Here is the number to a water damage cleaner; they do a wonderful job, and they don't overcharge." He handed me a slip of paper with their name and number.

"Thank you."

I called Paul, and he showed up in five minutes. He got a statement from the plumber and told me to give a copy of the report to the insurance adjuster, who arrived next.

"Babe, I'm so sorry about your place. Who would do this?"

He was mad now.

"I don't know, Paul. I don't have any enemies. Do you think maybe kids did this? Those teens I was telling you about."

"Maybe!" But he didn't look convinced.

I was so bummed out; I hated the fact that now I would have to cancel the Winter Ball! So many people were going to be disappointed.

"I have a lot of calls to make; I have to let everyone know that I'm canceling the event."

"Wait, just give me a minute, ok."

Paul dialed a number on his phone and called in a favor. I had a glimmer of hope!

"Hi, Mrs. Peters, it's Paul Anderson. I've been better, but thank you. I was wondering if you have any available rooms for about 250 guests. The Winter Ball that was going to be held at Kendle's will have to be canceled due to a broken water main, unless we have another location to have it. Oh, you bought some tickets, and you were going to attend, yes, I know it's the event of the year, yes, I was going as well.

You can, oh, thank you, Mrs. Peters, you're a lifesaver. I'll have Nikki call you and set everything up. Thank you again."

Paul hung up the phone.

"It's all set, you have the Ballroom at the Huntington."

He smiled, no doubt proud of his save of the day.

"Oh my gosh, you wonderful man, you are my Superman, I can kiss you!"

I kissed him on both cheeks and then one big one on the lips.

"How did you do that?"

"Mrs. Peters is the wife of one of the Lieutenants at the station, and she adores me! She gave Diaz and Lindsey a great deal on the room for the wedding, too! Plus, she had purchased tickets, so she was looking forward to coming this evening."

"She adores you, again, should I be jealous?"

I smirked teasing

"She's 62 and a grandma."

"Well, you know 62 is still glamorous, it's the new 30."

"Don't worry, she loves her husband."

"This is wonderful! I have calls to make to tell everyone we have a venue change. Thank you, Paul. I owe you."

"I can think of a few ways you can pay me back." He smacked my bottom with his clipboard and smiled foolishly.

"Don't get fresh!"

He embraced me again, and we kissed.

"Nikki, the insurance company needs the police report number," Daisy asked from inside the back doorway.

"Ok, I'll be right there, just give me a minute."

"I'll pick you up at 6 tonight."

"I'll see you later." I smiled.

I called Roxi and then Martin and Oliver after I dealt with the insurance company.

"Nikki, I'll be there to help. I'm on my way," Roxi said.

Martin and Oliver came by to help, too.

"Nikki, tell us what to do. We are here to help."

"Thank you, guys."

I divided up the guest list, and for the next hour, we were allowed to go upstairs to work in the office. Daisy, Tito, Oliver, Roxi, Martin, and I made calls to tell the guests briefly what had happened and why the venue had changed.

The cleaners pumped out the water, and thankfully, I was able to get them here today.

My devoted servers came in early and moved the tables, chairs, and furniture outside into the chilly air. While clean-up was in play. I had some movers pack up the restaurant furniture that was outside into a storage unit down the street.

After our calls, I called my buddy, the general manager at In-N-Out, and ordered some burgers, fries, and drinks. We turned on the heaters on the patio and sat down to lunch.

I had enough for everyone: the cleaners, the movers, the staff, the insurance adjuster, the plumbers, and my friends. Everyone was grateful and sat down for a much-needed break. Roxi put on some Christmas music that piped out to the patio.

"Santa Claus is Coming to Town."

We all started singing with joy and laughter.

"MERRY CHRISTMAS, EVERYONE!"

The Santa Streaker ran by, and we all laughed and yelled Merry Christmas. He ran in the other direction with a large smile on his face!

Chapter 16

Winter Wonderland

It was 4:30 pm, and the crew finished all of the cleanup, the plumbers fixed the pipe, and the serving staff had cleared out all of the furniture in the restaurant and my office.

The kitchen staff cleared out all of the food and equipment in the kitchen.

The movers had put everything in storage: the furniture, the heaters, and the patio furniture as well.

All of the food went to the hotel on a truck that the Huntington sent; just this once, they allowed outside food due to the circumstances.

Mrs. Peters was a gem, and I couldn't wait to meet her. I was beyond grateful to everyone in the community for all of their help. At the end of a very long day, I locked up the empty restaurant and headed home.

***

Jessica had picked up my dry cleaning.

Martin had called her to let her know what happened, and she wanted to do something to help after her shift ended at 4 pm. She came right before I locked up, and she couldn't believe the damage. "Nikki, this is awful. Who would do something like this?" Jessica asked.

"That's what we're all wondering, especially today, with the Winter Ball," Martin told her.

"I don't know, Nikki, this seems like it's personal. I know you think it's kids or teens, but something is giving me the vibe. I just don't know what I'm vibing."

Oliver put in.

"The thing is, maybe the pipe was old, or maybe it was someone who wanted to break into the place to get out of the cold," Martin suggested.

"There have been a lot of break-ins since the weather has become so cold."

I said.

"I'm with Oliver; this seems personal. Just watch your back, girlfriend."

Jessica replied.

We all headed out, the wind swelled up, and I cranked the heat in the car! I got home, indulged in a nice bubble bath, and then got ready. I paired my red dress with some black heels, a black clutch, and some gold earrings. I let my long locks down, my butterfly hair cut in curls, and waves cascading down my back.

Paul picked me up at six, right on the dot!

"You look beautiful; I'm going to have the best-looking date there."

"Thank you. You look handsome in that tux."

"You had to make it a formal dance, well, I'll be like all of the other guys there."

"Oh, no, you're not like all of the other guys." I kissed him.

He helped me with my coat, and then we left.

"You had to have a truck, didn't you?"

I opened the truck door and asked him for help getting in.

"That's right, trucks sit much higher than sedans."

I gave him my hand while I pulled myself in with the other hand. Thankfully, my long dress had a long slit on the side, so even though my leg was exposed, I didn't rip my dress.

"Very nice,"

Paul said, smiling with a devilish grin.

He closed the door for me and then hopped in the driver's seat, and we were off!

The Huntington was so beautiful, and here we were again, coming to another party. Paul valeted the truck so we wouldn't have to walk, but just go right into the hotel entrance. We made our way to the room, and I spotted a woman in a purple formal dress speaking to a banquet server. I bet this is Mrs. Peters.

"Oh, Paul, it's wonderful to see you, look at how nice you look, dear."

"Hi, Mrs. Peters, how are you this evening? This is my date, Nikki Rodriguez."

"It's wonderful to meet you." I extended my hand to her.

"Oh, it's nice to finally meet Paul's girl, you are a pretty one." She shook my hand.

"I'd like to thank you for all of your help and your staff. Please let me know what the total is for the staff and the use of the room."

"Oh my! No, this is a donation from the Huntington Group. I spoke to the board of directors, and when they heard what happened and that this is a charitable event, they simply decided not to ask for any compensation. It's Christmas, and so many of us still have the Christmas spirit; it's a time of giving."

I was so excited, my eyes watered.

"Thank you, I don't know what to say, Mrs. Peters, from the bottom of my heart, thank you."

"Think nothing of it, dear. Let's go in and let me know if the timeline of events is correct."

We went into the room, and the tables were decorated with white tablecloths and white napkins. The florist brought in the centerpieces that I had chosen for the tables, a large glass jar with candy canes lining it, and then a flower arrangement of white flowers, with ivy inside. They looked so cute and festive.

The Christmas tree became a backdrop for photos with lighting and a professional photographer stationed there.

The dessert table was decorated with pine cones and pine greenery. The sparkling white dance floor, with lights in red and green dancing above!

To the side of the room, the tables held the items for the silent auction going up for bid.

The dancers and entertainers were fully costumed and waiting to go on stage. It all looked so magical. The music played upbeat Christmas songs; now, the guests were beginning to arrive. Women were arriving wearing glamorous gowns in shades of emerald green, dark green, royal blue, gold, red, purple, cream, silver, and wine. The men were so dapper in their tuxedos; the staff had on our Christmas uniforms that we had at Kendle's.

As the hostess, I had to make my rounds to greet everyone; Paul came with me.

"Mrs. Green, you look lovely."

I admired her royal purple gown in silk.

"Nikki, I wouldn't have missed it." She hugged me.

"I'm so sad to hear what happened at Kendle's. Will everything be ok?"

" The contractor that came by said it would be a few weeks until everything would be ready, so they are looking at maybe late January to open back up! It needs new floors and some new baseboards; they said the drywall was salvageable, though, and everything in the kitchen was cleared to be saved! That's what the owners told me."

"That's at least good news! Paul, you need to find out who did this!" Mrs. Green stated to Paul.

"I'm on top of it, Mrs. Green. Trust me, when I find the person, I'm going to make sure they are prosecuted to the full extent of the law."

Guests were beginning to dance now, and the appetizers and drinks were being consumed.

I spotted Joanne and her husband Bob, Leslie Gray, and her plus-one. Craig and Kiana were there, too.

"Hi, you two look really nice."

Kiana hugged me, and Craig shook hands with Paul!

"I have a bid on those courtside VIP basketball tickets for the Lakers. Do you think I have a chance, Nikki?"

"Sure, Craig, remember if you have the highest bid, you win them."

"It's gonna be me!" He danced his little happy dance.

Kiana just rolled her eyes. "Come on, Craig!"

I spotted Roxi and her date. Paul and I walked over to them. Roxi had a pink gown on and her platinum blond hair in curls cascading around her shoulders. She looked absolutely beautiful.

"Girl, look at you in that red dress, what a beauty."

"Wow! You look incredible, too!"

"So, Paul, any word yet on who did this? Was it those kids that we think did the robberies?"

"No word yet, Roxi!"

"Soon!" She said and then led her date to the dance floor.

The mayor arrived next, along with Stacie Mc. Daniels, whom I might add, was dressed in a royal blue tight satin dress, which I thought had way too much cleavage showing for my taste.

Her high slit up the side of the dress was just as risqué. She glared down at me, her height of 5'10, towering over my 5'7 stature.

I shook Mayor CJ's hand and complimented her gown in light shimmering gold; it really was gorgeous.

"Ms. Mayor, you look absolutely stunning."

"Thank you, Ms. Rodriguez, you look amazing too!"

"Ms. Mc. Daniels, nice to see you again."

Paul was standing right next to me. He shook the mayor's hand and complimented her. When Stacie saw Paul, she ignored my greeting and went straight for him.

"Paul, it's so good to see you again!"

She came up to him and hugged him. Gracious as he was, he greeted her with kindness even when he noticed what she did and then diverted his attention to me.

"My Nikki has put together an amazing evening; I hope you both enjoy it. She is truly a wonderful woman."

I wanted to kiss Paul right here, but I didn't. I just smiled at him and said, "Thank you, Paul, you're amazing too!"

Stacie looked as if she wanted to explode; her eyes narrowed at me. She didn't say anything, and when Mayor CJ told her.

"Let's go find our table."

Her smile returned tenfold, and she said,

"Of course, everything looks fabulous."

They walked away in search of their seats.

Paul and I went to get some appetizers that were on a table by the bar; then we greeted more guests.

"Hey Paul, do you know that man over there? He looks familiar?"

Paul looked at a man in a green tartan tuxedo jacket and dark slacks.

He looked very festive and somewhere in his early 40s, if I had to guess. He looked athletic and healthy, with a full head of dark hair, hazel eyes, and a nice California tan.

Maybe he is a personal trainer or has a job that keeps him fit.

"No, Nikki, I've never met him before!"

I walked up to him and introduced myself

"Hi, I'm Nikki Rodriguez. I'm the hostess of tonight's events."

He smiled a big, jolly smile and replied: "It's nice to finally meet you, Ms. Nikki, my name is Nicky, too, just with a Y."

"Well, how do you do, Nicky? Are you new here in Rancho Niguel?"

"You can say I'm here on business, just for the holidays."

"Oh, ok, well, we have a wonderful evening planned!"

"It looks amazing already. It's so nice to see a community like Rancho Nigel. Why, since I've been here, I've seen decorations all over the city, community markets, carolers, churchgoers, bake sales, parades, and now this wonderful Christmas ball?

I am truly amazed, and it fills my heart with joy. You are very lucky to live here."

He was right. Rancho Niguel was a special place filled with community, friends, families, stores, restaurants, schools, churches, parks, and so much more. I was really lucky.

"Nikki, just keep doing what you are doing, and everything will work out."

"You're right." I smiled at him. Something about him was honest and sweet. A noble man, I thought.

"It's nice to meet you and get yourself a drink; they are free, it's an open bar. Please enjoy the festivities."

"Thank you." He replied.

"Oh, Nikki, I've been looking all over for you," Joanne said, tapping me on the shoulder. I turned to her and said,

"Have you met Nicky?"

"Who?"

"Nicky, he's right here!" I turned around, but Nicky was gone. I searched the room, but I couldn't find him. Oh well, maybe he high-tailed it to the bathroom.

"Uh, never mind! How are you doing?"

"I finally opened the store back up; I have no choice, this is my busiest season."

"I hear that."

After my brief discussion with Joanne, I had to excuse myself to go and give my speech for the silent auction.

I walked up to the makeshift stage at the front of the room and picked up the mic.

"Ladies and gentlemen, thank you all for coming to the annual Winter Ball." The applause was all over the room.

"Now, I'd like to have everyone take a look at these wonderful items and services to bid on for our silent auction. Remember, all of the proceeds go to charity at the Pediatric Wing in Rancho General Hospital. Just place your signature on the bidding sheet that is in front of the item you are bidding on.

We have some nice items up for auction, especially that beautiful 2023 Ducati Panigale V4 S Ducati Motorcycle in Red that has had a mob of men checking it out. Thanks to Ducati of Rancho Niguel for their generous motorcycle donation.

It will also be the only item we do a live auction with because of the open bid amount of $5000.00. Everyone, we want to get a large donation for the hospital, so pull out your credit cards, cash, or checkbooks and bid on these fabulous items and services.

Thank you, and remember, at 9:30 pm, we will close the bidding, and the winners will be declared.

Right now, I'd like everyone to take their seats. Dinner will be served, and we have an amazing show for you."

Once everyone made their way to their table, the servers came out with trays of dinner plates filled with Beef Wellington, fresh King Salmon, and some vegetarian options of vegetable pasta and mushroom risotto.

I sat down for dinner next to Paul and had a bite of the beef. So delicious. I went back to the mic and introduced the entertainment.

"For your entertainment this evening, welcome Group 45."

The stage lit up, and the musicians played the musical intro.

Dancers in extravagant holiday costumes in red, gold, green, and silver, feathers, rhinestones, and tap shoes filled the stage.

Male dancers in matching tuxedos danced with their leading ladies. The band played swing-style music from the 1940s and 1950s, some Christmas songs, and a mix of light jazz.

The dancers were so much fun.

I hired gals to circulate the room wearing old-fashioned costumes just like the cigarette and cigar gals used to wear in clubs during the 40s, 50s, and early 60s, but instead of selling nicotine, they passed out candy.

Red and green jelly belly candies, peppermints, and candy canes. When the dancers finished their act, I opened the dance floor up for free dance.

The band played some holiday jazz; many couples began slow dancing. Paul took my hand, and we made our way to the dance floor, too.

"I think the event turned out quite nicely. What do you think, Paul?"

"I think you did a fantastic job, even considering what happened to Kendle's. With short notice, Nikki, you pulled it off."

Paul embraced me.

"You are an incredible woman, Nikki Rodriguez."

By the end of the evening, we had read the winners of the silent auction.

Craig won his Lakers VIP tickets, and Mrs. Green won the gift basket from Coco Jo's, a Staub cocotte in dark green with matching silicone utensils and cream-colored kitchen towels with green pine trees on them. Roxi won the Tattoo package from Get Inked, our local tattoo parlour.

Then, it was time for the big event!

"Ladies and gentlemen, now it's time to start the bidding on the 2023 Ducati Panigale V4 S Ducati motorcycle in a beautiful fire engine Red!" Roxi handed out paddles to guests who wanted to bid on the motorcycle. Once everyone had a paddle, I opened the bidding.

"Ok, ladies and gentlemen, the bid opens at $5000.00. Do I have five? ok, how about 10? Ok, how about 15 right back there, ok?" The bids were going up; it was at 20k, and now just Paul and a woman, and James Tank were in the running.

"How about 23k?" The gal dropped her paddle, disappointed. Now, Paul and James were down to the wire.

"25k, ok 27k 30k!" Paul put down his paddle.

"It's all yours, James."

James Tank had his phone with him; he was speaking to someone, and then his paddle went up.

"Sold to James Tank for 30K!" Everyone clapped and cheered. It was the largest donation this evening.

I walked over to James.

"James, congratulations, you are the highest bidder this evening. Enjoy that beautiful motorcycle."

Paul congratulated James and gave him a high five.

"Enjoy it, buddy."

The look on James' face was a little uneasy, almost like he felt bad for winning it from Paul.

"Well, ladies and gentlemen, I'm going to close the event with a song. Everyone, have a Merry Christmas, and I wish you all good tidings and joy."

The band began the intro, and I sang, "Have yourself a Merry Little Christmas."

I received applause, and I took my bow.

It was a magical evening.

Chapter 17

Christmas Eve

Last night's event was all over the Rancho Niguel Courier, with photos and many more photos of the Winter Ball.

The highlights of the story mentioned to me as follows: "The hostess of the evening, beautiful and radiant Ms. Nikki Rodriguez, put together a most spectacular night of dinner, dancing, and a magical holiday show.

Next year's ticket sales are projected to double due to the magnificent turnout. Our new Mayor, Ms. CJ Groves, told the Courier that she had a wonderful time and expects more to come next year.

"Congratulations, Ms. Rodriguez, on a job well done!" Was the mayor's quote.

I felt pretty good after reading this article; I would have to get the group together and make some plans for next year's event.

I finished up my coffee and decided I needed to run to the grocery store to get a few last-minute items for my Christmas dinner tomorrow evening.

The weather outside certainly looked frightful, brrr...

I opted for some flannel-lined jeans and a thick red sweater, my Ugg boots, and a hat; I grabbed my Home Alone moose beanie.

I got into the bug and cranked the heat! I parked in the second spot from the entrance to Sprouts Market.

I ran inside with my reusable shopping bags, grabbed a dark green cart, and headed for the deli.

I found the round of brie cheese I needed. There were many different kinds of crackers and spreads set out, so I opted for two different kinds of crackers and two types of spread, one fig and orange, and one pepper!

"It looks like someone is making her famous baked Brie." I turned around to find Matt behind me. Dressed in plain clothes, Jeans, and a sweater.

" What are you doing here? I thought you were working."

"One of my Lt.s wanted New Year's Eve and New Year's Day off, so I traded shifts with him. I'm taking today and tomorrow off."

"Now you can come to Christmas dinner; everyone will be there."

"I'm looking forward to it. Is there anything you need me to bring?"

"Oh my gosh," he caught me off guard. I thought for a brief second, and then I came up with: Uh, how about pies? Mrs. Green is bringing a dessert of some kind, a brownie cake thing, but I think having a variety of desserts would be nice, so maybe a Pecan pie and an Apple crumble pie sounds good."

"Ok, I will take care of that. I read about the Winter Ball in the paper this morning, though the photos were better online. You looked beautiful in that red dress; I'm sorry I had to miss it. I also heard about that Ducati someone purchased."

"Ha ha, oh, all of the men there were drooling over it! A few ladies placed a bid, too, but James took that one home. I'll have to ask Roxi how he paid for that. Was it cash, credit, or a certified check?"

"I heard it was all in cash, 100-dollar bills," Matt said.

I chuckled, thinking about James bringing in his cold cash.

"Oh my!"

Matt walked with me while I found the items for my dinner. We talked about Kendle's and the water break; I told him I think kids probably did that. He thinks it was personal.

"You've been talking to Oliver, haven't you!"

"All he said was that he thinks someone has it out for the owners of Kendle's."

I still hadn't told Matt that the owner of Kendle's was me. I don't know why I didn't tell him yet; many of my close friends knew: Tito and Daisy, Roxy, Paul, Martin, and Oliver.

"My money is still on someone breaking in," I replied.

Matt picked up four pies from the bakery and put them in the cart. We got to the register, I paid for my things, and he paid for the pies. He helped me put the groceries in my car and then said he had a few things to finish getting for tomorrow.

"Well, darlin', how about I leave these pies with you? It might be a little hard for me to drive home with them."

He told me, placing them in my mini trunk.

"What do you mean? Where is your truck?" I asked, looking around the parking lot now. The only thing I spotted was a red Ducati, just like the one from last night's auction.

I turned to see Matt put on a black Dainese motorcycle jacket with a red triangle on the front of it that looked like a devil, but it was actually called a speed demon.

He put on black leather gloves with strong knuckle protectors and a red and black AGV Italian full-face helmet. He got on the motorcycle next, took the key out of his jacket pocket, and put it in the ignition.

I was shocked!

"Am I missing something here? What are you doing with James' bike? Were you holding that helmet the whole time inside?"

I asked, looking like I was being punked.

He had his visor up so I could see him. He smiled.

"I sure was! Darlin', don't worry, this isn't James' motorcycle, it's mine!"

It took me a few seconds, but I figured it out when James was on his phone; he was conversing with Matt! Wow, sneaky!

"It was you on the phone with James; he was bidding for you!"

I announced, pointing a finger at him.

"That's right!" Mr. Slick smiled at his undercover scheme.

"I didn't know you rode. When did this happen?"

My hands on my hips now.

"I rode when I was young, and last year, I got my motorcycle endorsement, and now I have the motorcycle of my dreams."

I guess there were still things about Matt I didn't know.

The chill in the air was too much now; I was getting too cold, and I was worried about Matt riding on this beautiful piece of machinery.

I put my hands on his shoulders and told him.

"Matthew Stevens, you be careful on this motorcycle, do you hear me? I don't want to go to your funeral!"

He put his arms around me and hugged me.

"Don't worry. I'm always alert, and I follow all of the laws on the road."

I walked back to my car, and he started up the motorcycle and shouted.

"I'll see you in church tonight." He put down his visor, waved, and rode off.

I got in the car, still surprised by his little scheme, and went home.

Chapter 18

It Came Upon A Midnight Clear

After I put away the groceries, I sat down on the couch and dialed Roxi's number.

"She answered on the second ring.

"Hey, Nikki, what up, girl?"

"Oh my God, Roxi, you are never going to believe this. Matt is the one who purchased the motorcycle last night."

"What! I thought James bought it. He gave me cash last night, he had me go to the fire station, and then he gave me a small black case filled with stacks of $100. I was like, Where did you get this? Did you rob a bank? He told me he has been saving all of his money for a while now."

I took the case, and then I deposited the money into the charity account this morning."

I told Roxi what happened at Sprouts, and she laughed; she thought it was sneaky.

"That's what I thought too!"

I had a buzz on my phone

"Roxi, I have another call coming in. Can you hold on?"

"Sure"

I clicked over the next line.

"Hello."

"Nikki, this is Father Riley. I was wondering if I could have a moment of your time."

"Of course, is everything ok for tonight?"

"Oh yes, that's fine, this is about another matter. Can you come to the church in, say, fifteen minutes?"

"I'll be there."

"Thank you, Nikki, I'll see you then."

I clicked over.

"Roxi, I have to run to St. Mark's right now. I'll catch up with you tonight, ok."

"Ok, Nikki, see you in church."

I arrived at the church; it was empty except for Father Riley and a young man in a letterman's jacket from West Rancho Niguel High School that I recognized.

"Nikki, thank you for coming."

He pointed to a pew for us to sit down, the teen followed us, and Father Riley introduced him.

"This is Zack Hughes; he and his family have been coming to St. Mark's since he was baptized here as an infant."

"How do you do, Zack?" I said, shaking hands with him.

He seemed quiet and sad, a look of disappointment on his face.

"Nikki, the reason why I asked you here is for Zack; he has something to tell you."

Zack turned to me and took a deep breath; for him, it was now or never, and he went all in.

"Ms. Nikki, you see, I came to Father Riley for advice. I've always come here to the church with my family and to confession and Sunday school." He stopped but looked at Father Riley.

"Go ahead, Zack, it's ok."

"Ms. Nikki, I was one of the kids who robbed Coco Jo's and Lady Grays's tea shops. I didn't want to! I was forced to do it. This kid at school, named Lex, said if I didn't do it, he would hurt me." He said.

He was remorseful that I could see; it must have weighed heavily on him to confess because he kept clasping his hands together and folding them as if he was putting on hand cream. Nerves, that was my guess.

I looked to Father Riley, and he shook his head, yes, to assure me Zack was telling the truth.

Zack continued his story.

"Lex told me and Katy that he wanted us to check out the store first, and he told us what to look at, those expensive pots and knives and those tea kettles at Lady Grays that were fine china. He gave us boxes to put the stuff in, and we loaded them in this van, but first, he had Chucky, one of the computer kids, disarm the two alarms for us, and then we went in there, four of us that did the robbery. The other kids were too scared to say anything, but I couldn't keep this to myself; I felt so guilty! I had to do the right thing, so I came to Father Riley."

"Zack, why did Lex want you to do this?"

"Lex's family is the Biltmore family, you know, the ones that own those big cranes that are used to build tall buildings. He is mean and rich and just does this to get his kicks, to see if he can get away with it. He's a real bully. This is the third high school he's been to; he even got kicked out of some fancy school in Los Angeles because he put a guy in the hospital with broken bones by pushing him off a scaffolding."

Zack was scared, and I knew everything he told me was true.

"Zack, I have a friend who is a police officer. Would you be willing to talk to him?"

Zack looked at Father Riley.

He nodded at Zack.

Ok, Ms. Nikki."

I called Paul and relayed the conversation to him about what Zack told me.

"He's on his way," I said after I hung up the phone.

When Paul arrived, we went over the whole story again. Zack was feeling more confident and agreed to give a statement.

"Officer Anderson, I just want you to know I will do all I can to prevent Zack from going to Juvenile Hall. He's a good boy, and the church will stand by him all the way."

"Ok!"

Paul made a call and then told Father Riley and Zack to come to the station. A car was sent to pick up Lex and question him at the station. "I'll have you in two separate rooms; he won't know you are even there."

"I'm going to!" I volunteered.

When we got to the station, Father Riley, Zack, and I went into a room. We could see the interrogation room by way of the two-way mirror.

An officer brought in Lex, who was a tall, heavy-set kid who looked like he could play for the Los Angeles Rams. He took a seat with an older man, probably his father, and another man dressed in a business suit sat next to them, a lawyer!

That is what I assumed. Paul and Craig came in with a folder and sat across from them.

The room was pretty fancy, I thought; it looked just like a small boardroom in light gray.

A table that sat six, black wood folding chairs, silver light sconces, and a framed photo of the Rancho Niguel police department seal. We had audio in the room, too. Sonya walked in and told us they were ready. She pushed a button so we could hear what they were saying.

Lex looked like he didn't have a care in the world. He sat in the chair with a smirk and an attitude that said You're wasting your time.

"Lex, I'd like to ask you if you know anything about the robberies that took place on December 21?" Craig asked.

Lex looked at his lawyer.

The lawyer responded, "Lex wasn't in the area; he was with his family at a cabin in Lake Arrowhead."

"I didn't ask where he was, I asked if he knew about the robberies?" Craig repeated.

The lawyer replied, "Lex doesn't know. We are here as a courtesy."

"I'd like to know why Lex has been to three different schools. Is it because of bullying?" Paul asked.

Lex's face changed, and now he looked worried.

"Lex has never been charged with anything. Move on!" The lawyer replied.

"We have witnesses who stated Lex was in charge of the robbery and set it up."

"That's nonsense!" Lex's father shouted.

"Do you want to tell us what happened, Lex? Now is your chance."

"Don't say anything, Lex." His lawyer instructed.

There was a knock at the door, Paul got up and opened the door, took the file another officer handed him. The officer told Paul something, and Paul looked like he had solved the puzzle.

He closed the door again and went back to the table, showed Craig the file, and then again asked Lex.

"This is your last chance, Lex. If you come clean, we can make a better deal."

"We are done here, detective. My client hasn't been charged, you have no proof, and we are leaving."

"Not so fast, we had a search warrant signed by a judge earlier, we were let in by your wife, Mr. Biltmore, and we found all of the stolen items in your garage."

Lex began to weep.

"I'm sorry, Dad, I did it, I was trying to show you I was able to lead and get something done."

"Your mom told us you weren't at the lake house that night!" Craig told him.

"She's not my mother, she's just another woman my dad married, what number is she, dad number five? I can't keep track anymore. I don't get any attention from you, you don't ask me about school, and you don't care that I'm always falling behind. You don't care about me."

Mr. Biltmore was looking like he had never known this. I found that hard to believe. The lawyer shouted, "I need a moment with my client."

Paul and Craig walked out of the room. Sonya turned off the sound and turned to us. "He has to converse with his lawyer, so we should go and wait in the break room."

We followed her out and had some hot chocolate and cookies in the staff break room.

After about an hour, Paul came back and gave us the update.

"Lex copped to everything, he said he gave the orders and threatened all of the other kids with harm if they didn't do what he said. He was right, the father is always away on some business trip, and his stepmom ignores him; his real mom died when he was 10, and he's always alone in the house. The only people he sees regularly are the housekeepers and the chauffeur. Poor kid, I feel sorry for him! But it looks like he will be in Juvi for a few months, and he has 200 hours of community service. If he goes to mandatory counseling, he might pull through. At least that's what the DA is offering."

"A troubled young man, I will pray for him." Father Riley said. "Zack, the DA said you and your friends will get misdemeanors for trespassing, and you can do 25 hours of community service. Your parents and your school would like you all to get some counseling for the bullying."

"I can do that." Zack agreed.

Father Riley was satisfied with the outcome and said he would see us in church tonight. Zack and his parents went home.

"It's all in a day's work, huh!"

"Yup!"

Paul and I went back to my place; I made some Mexican rice. Then I heated the tamales from Rosies Tamale House in LA, and two Modelo Negro beers.

We had dinner and turned on the fireplace. We discussed a little bit of the case and then decided to get some shut-eye.

"Dress warm this evening, Paul."

"Ok, I'm going home to get a few hours of sleep, and I'll pick you up at 11:30!"

"Ok, see you then."

I put on my jammies, set my alarm for 11, and I was out.

By the time he picked me up, the temperature outside read 32 degrees.

We arrived at St. Mark's on time, Paul and I picked a seat next to Martin and Oliver, and Mrs. Green was behind them with Jessica and Roxi. Matt came in and sat next to Roxi. Mass began, and Father Riley gave his opening speech about giving and the spirit of the true meaning of Christmas. Toward the end of mass, I walked up to the altar. Father Riley handed me the mic, and I began my song "Oh Holy Night." With the help of the church children's choir singing the melody.

After my song, Father Riley came up with me, I handed him the mic, and he blessed everyone and said, "Merry Christmas."

The doors opened and we saw snow falling. Everyone went outside to witness the peaceful scene.

Next to me, a gentleman dressed in a blue suit named Nicky said, "It's the true meaning of Christmas, never forget it."

Paul, Roxi, Mrs. Green, Jessica, Martin, Oliver, Father Riley, Matt, and the rest of the midnight mass congregation agreed with Nicky. He walked away and shouted **MERRY CHRISTMAS, EVERYONE,** he ran down the street and then disappeared.

"Was that?" Martin asked, but Roxi shouted.

"That was the Santa Streaker!"

"No, that was the Christmas Angel, a messenger from above." Father Riley smiled. He crossed himself and walked back into the church.

We all just stood there, freezing our bottoms off, trying to make some sense of it all. Then we all smiled and said Merry Christmas. There were hugs all around, and even Matt and Paul shook hands and wished one another a Merry Christmas. The snow came down faster now! Roxi turned to me.

"Nikki, it looks like Rancho Niguel is having a White Christmas."

Chapter 19

Christmas Day

I woke up at about 10 or 11 am, and I was ok with it. Last night was wild, it was probably the most interesting Christmas Eve I've ever had!

I called my mom and Jeff to wish them a Merry Christmas; they were skiing in Aspen. They asked me to come every year, and I told Mom that next year I would definitely go. I told them what happened Christmas Eve at church, and they were impressed.

I turned on the TV and watched Christmas Vacation while I started some food prep. I popped a tamale in the microwave and snacked on that for breakfast with a cup of coffee. Roxi called me and said she and her boyfriend were going to get a ride from Matt, who has a 4x4, so getting through the foot of snow would be easy. Jessica just lives in the next complex over, and she has a Subaru Forester, so she said it would be no problem getting here. Paul has his truck and everyone else invited lives here, so my dinner is still on for tonight. Paul said he would come over early to give me my Christmas present.

I couldn't wait, I bought him a surfboard and two tickets for us to fly to Hawaii in the spring.

I opted for a pair of black slacks and a long-sleeved red blouse. I put on some gel-soled flats for pure comfort.

Around 4 pm, I had the table nicely set with a red table runner down the middle, place settings for each person, and two centerpieces of tea lights in clear bowls with water in them, a floating candle look. My fireplace was on and filling the condo with warmth. Paul arrived, and he came in with a bag with four different wines. "I brought red, white, rosé, and sparkling cider."

"Oh, that's perfect."

He put all of the wine and beverages in the kitchen. I had his board leaning in the hallway, with a nice big green ribbon around it.

"This is for you." He handed me a square box wrapped in green paper with moose and Santa hats and a big white ribbon on top. I removed the wrapping paper and opened the white box.

"Oh, this beautiful Paul! A diamond tennis bracelet!"

"I knew you didn't have one, so I thought this would be right."

I kissed him. "I love it, thank you." He helped me put it on, and it sparkled in the light of the fireplace.

"Ok, now it's your turn."

I grabbed his hand and led him into the hallway

"Close your eyes."

We were standing in front of it now! "Open your eyes!"

"Oh wow, a new board. A Chemistry surfboard, wow, these guys are based in Oceanside."

"Yes! Roxi and I drove down last month to get it."

"I love it, I can't wait to try it out!"

"Well, it might be a few weeks."

"Now this next gift is for both of us."

I handed him the envelope, and he opened it up. Two first-class tickets to Hawaii were inside. I had won two tickets from the raffle that Matt had entered me in back in late October. The tickets were two coach airfares, and the hotel was less than stellar, so I upgraded to first class. No compact sedan for us, I ordered the jeep and changed the hotel to a beachfront five-star resort. I admit I like rock star vacations with all of the trimmings. I didn't spare any expense on this one.

"What! No way! We are actually going?"

"Yes, and I even checked out the charges for taking our boards too!"

"This is too much, oh Nikki! We're going to have a blast."

He was like a little kid, now excited and full of smiles.

The guests arrived an hour later, everyone came in with their white elephant gift, and they were placed under the tree.

"Oh, Craig, I hope you didn't get a box of extension cords like last year." Mrs. Green said.

"Don't worry, Mrs. Green, I bought the gifts this year," Kiana replied.

"Nikki, where is your lighter? The candles went out."

"In the drawer next to the desk, Roxi."

We all sat at the table now. I was at the head of the table, and to my right sat Matt, Roxi, and her boyfriend, Jessica, and then the end cap had Mrs. Green, Craig, Kiana, Martin, Oliver, and then Paul next to me on my left.

We said a nice prayer and then everybody dug right in. We had glazed ham, roasted beef tenderloin, Brussel sprouts with bacon, candied sweet potatoes, Roxi's scalloped potatoes, a charcuterie board, bacon-wrapped scallops, Mrs. Green's mudpie brownie, pecan pies, and apple streusel pies. We also had my Brie cheese and Jessica's cheese ball. I think we had enough food for the next couple of days.

Dessert came, and dessert went; there were only two slices of pie left and one piece of mudpie.

I put all of the dishes in the sink and started to wash them, and everyone pitched in, and in 20 minutes, we were done. We all moved to the living room for the white elephant.

"Ok, everyone draws a number out of the Santa hat.

"Jessica got number one; she picked a shiny gold package. She opened it up, and it was a four-pack of toilet paper, but taped to the side was an envelope with $80.00 inside. "I'll keep this one." She smiled.

Next was Craig; he stole Jessica's gift, and then she had to get another. She got a gift card for $75.00 from Macy's.

"This works for me."

Matt unwrapped a Mickey Mouse cookie jar filled with $1.00 bills, and Mrs. Green ended up with two tickets to see a musical. She was pretty jazzed about it. Roxi got a tacky ashtray with $100.00 taped to the bottom of it. Her boyfriend got a basketball with two Lakers tickets. I ended up with a jar of peppermints and a gift card to Coco Jo's for $100.00, cool. Paul got a Dodger cap with two tickets to the Dodger game in April. Kiana got a set of wine glasses with a wine of the month club, Oliver ended up with a pair of Gucci sunglasses, and Martin got the best prize, two days at the Hotel Del Coronado in San Diego.

"What, who bought that gift?" Roxi asked.

"I don't know, but we're going to enjoy it."

Martin replied, holding the tickets close.

When we all had gifts, there were a few more takes and trades, but everyone was laughing and having fun.

After the gifts, I guess everybody got a second wind, and now Cokes were being popped open, more glasses of wine were poured, and two buckets of popcorn made their rounds.

Craig started a game of 21, and now half of the group was playing cards, the other half was talking, and all of us were watching bits of A Christmas Story on TV.

Paul was showing Martin and Roxi his new board.

Matt followed me to the kitchen to get some water.

"I wanted to give you this away from everyone else."

He handed me a box wrapped in paper with moose and Santa hats.

I guess this wrapping paper was the man's choice roll.

I smiled to myself.

I opened the box. A gold necklace with a gold treble clef in diamonds.

"Oh, Matt, this is so beautiful."

"Allow me," he asked, taking the necklace in his hands.

I pulled my hair up, and he placed the necklace around my neck.

"It's a good thing I didn't opt for the tennis bracelet; you would have had two."

"Thank you again, I love it." I hugged him.

"Wait, just one second, I have something for you."

I went to my room and grabbed a red envelope.

I walked back to the kitchen and handed it to Matt.

"Here you go, I hope you like it." I smiled.

He opened the envelope and pulled out two tickets to the Boys of Country, VIP backstage passes.

"What! How did you get these? They've been sold out! One night with some of the best acts in country music: Tim McGraw, Kenny Chesney, Clint Black, George Straight, Toby Keith, and Vince Gill. All on one stage. I get to meet all of these guys?"

"Yeah, you do, VIP backstage passes," I said, smiling and nodding yes.

"Oh, baby, come here, thank you, this is wonderful."

He gave me a big hug.

"There are two tickets here. Are you going with me?"

"Maybe."

"Ok, you and me, April 22"

"It's on," I replied.

We went back into the living room, played a few games, laughed some more at the movie, and then by 10:30 pm, we called it a night.

Paul was the last one here with me; we sat in front of the fire listening to Christmas tunes that were playing.

 "Baby It's Cold Outside."

"That's an understatement," Paul said.

He soon fell asleep. I removed his shoes and covered him with a blanket, "Merry Christmas, Paul," I whispered to him. I kissed his cheek, and I went to my room to bed.

Chapter 20

New Year's Eve

I packed a weekend bag with all of the things I would need up in the mountains. The snow had stopped the day after Christmas, and now it was all melted. Up in the mountains, it was still there, so we would be taking Paul's car to get up to Big Bear.

Tito and Daisy decided on a small wedding at an Inn up in Big Bear next to her family's cottage. She asked me to be her maid of honor, and I happily said yes.

The wedding was taking place at 11:50 pm, right before midnight. I booked two rooms at the Inn for Paul and me for a two-night stay. The rates were pretty reasonable, I thought, and it would give us a chance to do some sledding and possibly some skiing.

Paul picked me up at 3 pm, right on time, and we were off. The roads were a little busy; many Southern Californians were crazy about the snow and were trying to get their fill of it.

"You seem pretty quiet. What's going on?" Paul asked me.

"I'm thinking we had a December for the record books."

"It's been pretty wild."

"I have some good news, I spoke to Jeff, my stepdad, and it looks like he's going to make the Youth Center happen."

"Oh, that's wonderful, wow, thank you."

"I had Betty Jean look into some places that are up for lease, and if there is nothing out there, then we can build something."

"Hopefully, we can find a building so that we can get it up and running faster."

"Exactly my point, Betty Jean is good at her job, she'll find what we need, I'm confident."

We arrived at the Inn, and it was more than I expected. The mountains were snowy with the bright sun shining above.

The Inn had a large covered driveway, and the bellhops and valets stood at the ready. We valeted the truck and went into the Inn. The inside was warm, and the large stone fireplace filled the lobby with heat. We checked in and then took the large staircase to the second floor. Rooms 217 and 219 were located at the end of the hall, with a view of the mountains and the lush gardens. The rooms had a large jetted tub and a minibar filled with goodies, usually overpriced. There was a large gift basket with Champagne and chocolates in my room on the dresser. The card on it had our names written in calligraphy. *Nikki and Paul*

It was from Daisy and Tito thanking us for coming. Included was the wedding program and things to do. Paul and I had a few hours until tonight's event, so we decided to go sledding.

The lines were long, but we waited anyway. We were dressed in snow gear and boots. When our turn came up, we sat together in the large inter tube, held on tight, and went down the hill.

We had so much fun, we went three more times. After that, we grabbed dinner and then went back to our rooms to get ready for the wedding. Daisy had gone with long black velvet for the maid of honor and bridesmaids' dresses, and since it was just me and her two cousins, it made it easy. I put on my high-heeled boots that went just below my knee. Stylish and it would keep my legs warm. I had a faux black stole fleece-lined to go with it to place around my shoulders.

We walked down to the small banquet room for no more than 40 guests, which was decorated very beautifully. The room had high open ceilings with wood beams. Another stone fireplace, but not as large as the one in the lobby. The chairs were set out for 35 guests for the ceremony, and the two round tables were set behind the ceremony area. White lights were all over the room, and a Christmas tree sat in a corner by the small bar. The DJ set up in the opposite corner of the room near the small dance floor.

Daisy was in the bride's room just outside the banquet room. I told Paul I would see him in a few minutes.

In the dressing room, Daisy was just about ready. She had her sapphire hairpin in her hair, and she wore a long lace gown with lace sleeves and a white faux fur stole around her shoulders. She looked very glamorous and very happy.

"Hi Nikki, oh, you look beautiful, are your rooms ok?"

"Oh yes, everything is wonderful. You look amazing! Tito is going to be speechless."

We all walked out of the bridal room in the direction of the wedding coordinator at the Inn, "Ok, ladies, I'll have you line up here!"

We took our places, and we waited for the music to cue us, and then we began. We walked down the aisle to a light jazz song, we took our place in front of the guests, and then the big moment, Daisy stood at the end of the aisle, and when the music played Kenny G's "The Wedding Song," she began to walk down the aisle, her scarlet roses with ivy gave a contrast with her dress, she was radiant.

Tito was at the altar in his black tuxedo, looking like one happy dude.

The officiant smiled at both of them now as they joined hands.

"Welcome, family, friends, we are here today to join these two people, Tito Anthony Kingman and Daisy Elizabeth Carpenter, in matrimony." Tito and Daisy wrote their own vows.

"I take you, Daisy, to be my wife. I will love and care for you in sickness and in health, all of the days of your life. I give my love to you always." He placed the ring on her finger.

"I take you, Tito, to be my husband. I will love and care for you in sickness and in health, all of the days of your life. I give my love to you always. She placed the ring on his finger.

"I now pronounce you husband and wife."

"I'm gonna kiss the bride!" Tito shouted with gusto.

Everyone clapped and cheered for them.

The Clock in the room struck midnight, and everyone yelled Happy New Year! The DJ played the New Year's Eve Song. We all held our glasses of champagne, toasting one another and singing old acquaintances be forgotten... Paul planted a kiss on me, and we wished each other a Happy New Year!

Epilogue

January

So this is the new year, and I have high hopes and big plans. I have a list of things I'm going to accomplish, and I am ready to go! The new floors and the new baseboards were just put in; it looks like we will reopen in the next few days. I've decided to write a journal as a new way to release my thoughts and possibly give myself more insight into... Myself.

I closed my journal and stuck it on the shelf in my bedroom closet. December was a month for the books, and I can't say that I'm surprised.

Things in Rancho Niguel have been changing. Paul still didn't have any leads on who had tipped off the press to the siege on Vic! Plus, we still didn't know who had tipped off the press back in October about the information regarding the Vampire bites from Cat's murder! Not to mention, we still had no suspects for the water pipe break at Kendle's! Although there was good news from Paul! Last night at the chamber of commerce, honoring the winner of the highest charity donation from a Christmas Angel went to

Detective Paul Anderson. He garnered a surprise from everyone, especially Craig!

"Thank you to Kendle's Kannery Restaurant for their generous donation of $5000.00."

That was the speech Paul made when called up and asked to say a few words. So we would have that vacation in Hawaii come June! Reminiscing about the holidays is always fun. Now, I have a brand new year to expand my businesses and the band; the ladies are all over the flu, everyone is healthy, and we are ready to take on some new gigs. My stepfather, Jeff, loved the idea of having his money put into a new youth center. We opted for just the fund's donation; Jeff doesn't want his name on a building, he's too kind for that. He did, however, put me as a member of the board to oversee the facility. The board loved the idea and made me an offer to become a lifetime member. Stacie, however, wasn't a fan of my involvement, but it wasn't up to her. So the board decided to call it The Rancho Niguel Youth Center. I had some say in some activities and programs we would offer. Sports, cooking classes, art classes, music classes, tutoring for all grade levels, dance classes, computers, self-defense/Karate/Judo/Tae Kwon Do, fencing, fishing, auto mechanics, gardening, and some job training corps for the older teens.

It made my heart full to think of the benefits the community would have. Classes and tutoring are free, and the only thing required is attendance and finishing the classes.

Our donors became abundant and plentiful, thanks to Jeff's connections and his generous friends. Just maybe we can save kids from trouble on our streets and give them a direction to a wonderful future with family, friends, and community. I finished my cup of coffee, and I was just ready to head over to Kendl's to do some paperwork and manage for the next three evenings while Tito and Daisy took a week off for their honeymoon to Catalina Island. I grabbed my purse, put on a light jacket, and made my way out to the bug. I got in, turned on the radio to my favorite Pandora station, and then I got a call from Matt.

"Hey, dude, what's up?"

"Nikki! I need your help!"

"What's wrong, Matt?"

"I just got a call from my mom, my sister ran away!"

Don't miss the next exciting Nikki

Rodriguez adventure

Romance, Runaways, and

Rock n' Roll

Ah, the month of love! Valentine's Day is on its way! Tho all is not love in Rancho Niguel. When Matt's little sister runs away from home, Nikki volunteers to help find her before she gets into trouble. The new Youth Center is up and running, but is someone trying to sabotage Nikki's efforts? It's not all candy hearts and a box of chocolates when a local Rock n' Roll legend turns up missing after a big concert. Can Nikki find two missing persons, catch a vandal, and keep her boyfriend Paul away from his ex Stacie? It seems like only Cupid himself can bring love to Rancho Niguel.

ABOUT THE AUTHOR

M.A.Hansen

From a young age, M.A. Hansen has been writing short stories, poems, and novels for fun. This series is her first set of independently published books.
Her hobbies include reading mysteries, hiking, crocheting, and an infinite love of cooking and baking. M.A. spends her time in the PNW and in sunny Southern California with her wonderful husband of 30 years. She is a mother and now a grandmother.
"I hope you enjoy reading about the adventure with my character Nikki Rodriguez, a journey of love, mystery, and laughs."
M.A. Hansen